THE MIDNIGHT *WARRIORS*

NIRMANI WALPOLA

editors@emerald-books.com

BISAC Categories:

YAF056000   YOUNG ADULT FICTION / Science Fiction / General

YAF062020   YOUNG ADULT FICTION / Thrillers & Suspense / Espionage

Summary:

Clara, the most popular girl in school, and Damien, an antisocial prankster, have nothing in common except their friendship. But each of them withholds a secret from the other: they're both secret teenage assassins from the same organization. Follow Damien and Clara from their points of view as they balance their lives as regular middle schoolers with their sworn obligation to save the world.

ISBN: 978-1-954779-13-6

CONTENTS

DEDICATION

To my ever-loving grandparents, Acha and Seeya and Achiammi and Seeya, who have stood behind me the whole time I wrote this book: This one is for you.

CHAPTER 1

HISTORY PROJECT?
YOU CAN HAVE IT IF YOU LIKE

CLARA

If I had known that today I would have to save my best friend from being murdered by *the* most dangerous criminal leader in the world, I really wouldn't have gotten up this morning.

My alarm rang. I rolled over to see that it was four in the morning, the time when I'm supposed to wake up. I only slept for four hours, and I felt like absolute junk. Getting up this early is the worst—no matter how many times I've done it. I couldn't sleep in or snooze. In order to protect my secret, I *had* to get out of bed, I *had* to finish my homework, and I *had* to go to school.

I turned on my bedside lamp and covered it with a blanket. I quickly closed the dark curtains that hung from the ceiling 'cause I didn't want my mom to know I was awake yet. More importantly, I didn't want my dad to know.

I got out of bed and sat down at my old cedar desk. My mom had given it to me for my sixth birthday. It was the same one that she had as kid, but it was still in mint condition. Looking through my messy pile of papers, I found the exact thing I was hoping to avoid.

Other than birthday invitations, chocolate wrappers, and other crud, I had one important document, my history project rubric. My best friend since forever, Damien Richards, was my partner on the project. Mrs. Leborn assigned the project as 50% of our grade. The assignment was to write an autobiography and include a little bit about our family history. Easy enough, right?

I wish. Nothing's easy when you're a Lemondola.

And why didn't you do this? I asked myself. Oh, that's right. *Because you were busy texting Paulina, and you told yourself you would do it in the morning.*

I did convince myself to do it in the morning, since I was texting Paulina Demos, my closest friend since third grade, to help me with some math. She's in Algebra I, and I'm in a regular math class this year.

It was hard, and since my nights are occupied, I couldn't have her over for even a half hour.

Bad move, Clara. I could have kicked myself.

When I first got the project, I thought it wouldn't be *that* hard to write about myself. Now, I didn't know *what* to write.

Definitely not. "Hi! My name is Clarissa Aventurine Lemondola. My dad's one of the world's richest and nicest people, and I'm a hired assassin killing criminals with my mom. Yipee!"

It's not even funny, so don't try laughing. I really am an assassin. I'm not like the stereotypes you see in movies with the shady looks and bad catchphrases. Assassins (at least my kind) are always good, even though history (and everybody else in the world) portrays us as bad guys. Think of the saying "give a dog a bad name and hang him."

Who do you think came up with that?

I'm part of a group called ANW, or Assassins Nationwide, which takes in kids as young as five to be trained to target bad guys. Our targets are serial killers or other deadly trouble the world wants to get rid of. I better not tell you any more.

It wouldn't matter if I was her kid or not, my mom would kill me if I ever told anybody. ANW never tolerates this, not after—never mind. Just know that if there are bad people in history, well, let's just say they were taken care of, courtesy of us.

So how are people recruited? Good question.

My mom's whole family since the eighteenth century were ANW leaders. When I turn thirteen and complete the final level of my training, that responsibility will come to me.

So why let a teenager be in charge of a criminal organization?

3

The million-dollar questions just keep rolling in.

I could become a full leader if I wanted or I could wait until I'm eighteen. Besides, I still have non-assassin obligations ahead of me, like school and being a teenager. Anyway, the leader is responsible for choosing kids they think are worthy and teleporting them to the headquarters in Los Angeles, California, where I live.

Once you're teleported, if you like the organization and pass the trial, you are given the opportunity to join. If you don't want to join, you would be memory-wiped, and it would be like it never happened.

Well, not instantly. Each leader has a little tool for the purpose of erasing memory that is top secret. My mom would never let me use hers, since there are a couple people who I already knew I would want to use it on. My mom wasn't having that.

That part was creepy, but it was better than going up to a kid and saying, "Congrats, kid! You're an assassin. You've got ten minutes to decide if you want to accept this offer or you will be memory-wiped."

Once you're in, you get a uniform and weapons, and you start your training. I'll explain more in a bit.

When you turn thirteen, like I said before, you level up to become an "adult" assassin. You join a team with four other assassins you trust and go on missions with your team. I like that part the most.

The four assassins, roughly about the same age, are grouped together (after being watched carefully by the leader) and level up together. Then they work together and help each other.

As for me? I will level up just like everybody else, but before I officially can, I have to have my prophecy dream to confirm that I am the next ANW leader.

What's that, you say? It's...well...we'll cross that bridge when we come to it. I *really* shouldn't be telling you all of this. Some things are meant to be secret.

Believe me, I wish I could tell you everything.

Now, here's the twist: each ANW assassin has to wear an eye mask to cover their identity. You guessed it: you have no idea who the other people in your group are.

Hold up: I bet you're wondering what type of organization kills people without even knowing each other? Like my mom says, "It's for our own good." And for publicity.

There are assassin tribes all around the world who don't keep their identities secret, but Giovanna Lemondola, my great-great-great-great-grandma, created this organization 300 years ago, not to be a hero, but to make a change in the changing world.

We're only called by the first letter of our names until we get our codenames when we level up. For example, I'm called C, but my mom is known as Poppy, her codename. Like I said before, we wear masks, like the ones you would see at the carnival in Venice.

It's hard to recognize a masked person, trust me. When I was little, I would try to peel off another assassin's mask, but I swear, whatever glue they use doesn't come off! I wonder if they use Gorilla Glue...

Back to the history project.

My family? Easy. I am an only child, and I have no cousins. My parents are also only children, even though when I ask my mom about it, she just changes the subject.

A couple times, though, I have seen my mom finger a special rose-gold rose pedant, and softly cry over a photo with two girls around my age. The girl on the left has black hair, with a Cheshire cat smile. She's elbowing a blond-haired girl on the right, who just smiles knowingly at the other girl. The blond girl is my mom, so who was that black-haired girl, and why was she so important that my mom would cry over her?

That's suspicious. I don't ask about it, though, since assassins like to protect their privacy a lot. That's the number-one thing. My grandparents from my dad's side are alive, even though my mom's dad died when I was five. I have a few second cousins, but other than that, it gets lonely, to be honest.

Being an only child is not fun most of the time, especially when your dad's in charge of a multi-billion-dollar business, which means I only get to spend time with him on the weekends and, if I'm lucky, sometimes at night. When you're a billionaire's child, most people who seem to adore you are two-faced. One minute they'll be sucking up to you, and the next, they laugh you off like a day-old dirt sandwich.

But because of my mom and my friends Paulina and Damien, it isn't super-bad having no siblings. They make up for it 120%.

About myself? That's easy, too. I've lived in Los Angeles all my life, and I love anything sweet. I can get a sugar rush easily, so people keep their distance when I go with them to get ice cream.

I am considered popular, but only to anybody who doesn't know me personally. I honestly don't care, since I have friends and everything I need. I don't need much, and I like it that way. Also, being a billionaire's daughter is sweet (even with the struggles), and comes with many perks, like being invited to mingle with the rich and famous, even though I like peace and quiet most of the time. I have enough work to do every night.

Just as I was about to write about my ancestors, the door opened, and my mom came in. I ran to my bed and hid under my blanket. My mom chuckled.

"Clara, I brought some hot chocolate," she said as she tried to yank my covers off. "We had a late night," she acknowledged.

Don't remind me.

As a level two, I practice with everybody ranging from ten to twelve years old, girls and boys. I don't mind practicing with anyone except one person.

D.

Don't get me wrong. I'm good with most people, but there are some exceptions.

D joined at the same time I did, and my mom wanted us to get to know each other, so she paired us up. We were both only five, but for some reason, our tempers flared, and the next thing we knew, we were fighting. Ever since then, we've both made excuses to avoid fighting the other, and my mom doesn't say anything about it. I have a gut feeling she is keeping us from training together.

I really want to find out who D is, and maybe even be friends.

On second thought, no, I don't.

When my great-great-great-great-grandmother started this group, she obviously wanted to hide people so they wouldn't be targeted. So, she had the great idea of training people in the dead of night. Then, they could get stronger without enemies noticing.

Just wonderful for people who need to get some sleep in the 21st century.

Wait, did people actually get sleep before technology came around?

I perked up at the smell of my mom's homemade hot chocolate. It was a family recipe, and it made you feel like you could throw a car with one sip.

Of course, my mom won't share the recipe until I'm a leader.

Mom left the room and I sat up. I grabbed my phone and texted Damien.

If we didn't get an A on our history project, I would end up with a B as my final grade. Don't get me wrong—Bs are fine, but I really wanted to make my parents proud, even with my whole life turned upside down. I hoped Damien would get the message and try to finish his part of the project before it was due, or my grade was done before I could say "hot chocolate."

CHAPTER 2

DON'T PRANK YOUR LEADER

DAMIEN

I hid behind a small bush looking for someone. That someone's name was C. Top assassin and hit-girl of our level two class for kid assassins. That's what they call her. I call her a bunch of names, including Plastic, Princess Plastic, Whiner Girl, and some others that would get my throat slit if any adult heard me.

In our organization, recruits are only known by the first letter of their names. Let's just say that the first time we met, I ended up with a black eye and she ended up with a leg bruise. We were both five at the time, but she fought as hard as she does now. I remember going home with my whole head hurting once.

I honestly wonder how I keep this from my parents, especially when I come home visibly injured.

I saw C lurking about, looking for a sparring partner, but I had to stifle a laugh when I saw all the other assassins steered clear. They also knew her strength very well. Now that I think about it, the only other person who could beat her was our leader, Poppy.

Poppy (a codename) is a petite woman with delicate hands, but an attitude so strong, she would make all the Disney, Marvel, and Netflix villains cry. I'm pretty sure most of the cartoon villains are based on her. Most people who encounter Poppy at night don't live to tell the tale.

Poppy is C's mom, but I'm the only kid who knows that. I know for a fact that Clara is also here somewhere, but because of the rules ANW has, it's ridiculously hard to find anybody. Meanwhile, I started looking for C again, but she had mysteriously disappeared like she does every night. I tried following her once, but Poppy grabbed me by my shoes and told me to get back to work. She could flip a whole family and not break a sweat, but she just held me up by my shoes and turned me upside down. The whole world went flying, and I think I nearly threw up.

I really wonder how people deal with Poppy when she's *not* an assassin.

You're wondering, *What in the world is he talking about?*

I'm part of this secret organization that trains kids to be assassins. Yes, kids. It's called Assassins Nationwide, or ANW. That's all you will get out of me about our purpose... Coincidentally, ANW headquarters just had to be in the woods behind my house. There is a secret road that every assassin takes through the woods. Once you enter the woods, you walk in for at least 15 minutes, and you have

11

to watch out for booby traps. They're just the usual smoke bombs, mouse traps, and flying axes. Nothing an assassin can't handle.

It's just an extra precaution, since assassins are supposed to be up and ready at all times. When you finally enter the ANW headquarters, you come upon a ground filled with sand, like the floor of a Renaissance fair.

Around the arena, there are khaki tents everywhere filled with assassin kids and teenagers going in and out. These tents hold weapons, food, and other amenities. The tents are arranged in a U-shape, with Poppy's tent in the center. It's similar to a circus tent, and instead of khaki-colored, it's a deep royal purple.

Poppy's tent is the neutral ground of ANW headquarters, and it's like the counselor's office at school, except instead of comforting advice, you find axes and swords hanging across the walls.

If you exit the tent area, you get to the combat circle, which is where most assassins train and hang around. You see nunchucks, arrows, and black eyes there most of the time.

The last circle after the combat circle has two very special landmarks. One is a small white podium, and the other, a large tower. To me, it looks like a large wine glass, even though Poppy said it's "shaped like a golf tee," whatever that means. I have no knowledge when it comes to golf.

C's dad and my dad played golf almost every Sunday, and I was always there to pick up the balls and keep track of their scores. At first, being a gofer was fun, but that went downhill real quick.

I dodged a random sword and flipped over another assassin. Poppy interrupted the exercise and called to us. "Assassins! Older level twos! Make your way to the podium, now!" Half the kids on the ground ran to the podium. They ran toward Poppy, hoping to get a good spot near the front of the stage. "Level twos! Listen up! In a few days, everybody who is thirteen will be able to level up. Do you remember what you need to do?" Poppy asked, watching us like a hawk.

Most of the kids murmured a yes, or nodded, but I just sighed.

As Damien, I'd have to be silent. I had a reputation. As D, I was free to do anything. So, I did what any tired thirteen-year-old boy would do. Act stupid.

"Ummm, Poppy? What do we do? I only remember the part where we get to eat food." I acted as if Poppy hadn't repeated this for the fourth time, 'cause why not?

I am free.

The crowd snickered. Some just let out a low sigh. Some snapped their fingers to summon popcorn into their hands. They were ready to watch Poppy destroy me. Poppy slapped her hand against her forehead. "D! Listen up! Assassins, answer these questions for the knucklehead who didn't pay attention," she yelled.

"How long is the leveling up?" she asked.

"Five days!"

"What do you get?"

"Your special power and codename!"

"Do you understand now, *D*?" Poppy asked menacingly, almost as if she wanted to cover my mouth with duct tape.

I gulped. "Maybe?"

Poppy nodded and dismissed everybody. It was almost time to go home.

"Wait!" I called out.

"Any more questions?" Poppy said sharply.

"I might not...maybe don't...have a partner to spar with?" My voice squeaked.

Poppy held me up by my shoe again, and the blood rushed to my head.

"Anybody *not* have a sparring partner?" she yelled into the crowd.

Everyone stayed silent. Honestly? I wouldn't even pair up with myself. Even my shadow would beat me to pulp.

"I guess you can spar with me and rotate around with everybody else as we start. W, turn the radio on!" Poppy said.

As Poppy dropped me to the floor, a small sphere dropped out of my pocket. Before I had a chance to pick it up, it exploded into a nasty gas.

Curse my pranks.

Ever since I was born, my mom worried that I wouldn't be able to speak. And I didn't. She ran around to every doctor, psychologist, and therapist she could, trying to find a solution. One person, Dr. Gorgon, told her not to worry. He said that I just have a shy personality, and that I would start talking soon. He was right.

Even though I don't like *talking* to people, I love pranking them. I always carry an assortment of gags, pranks, and jokes. You name it, I got it. Of course, I only prank the people who need to be pranked. The usual harmless pranks (I'm not try to kill somebody here!) land on friends, and maybe my mom, who takes them lightly.

Here, though, I tried to run away, but Poppy grabbed me by the collar and gave a death stare that I could feel through her mask.

15

DAMIEN

"Mind explaining that to us?" Poppy asked.

I stayed silent, even though I was gagging inside.

You want the smell? Just think of a rotten corpse, melting in liquid garbage and dripping with flies. I actually caught the scent in a bottle during one of Poppy's impromptu classes, when we learned about identifying types of stenches. You wouldn't believe the types of dead bodies you can encounter. Maybe that's why I threw up for a week after the class.

"Poppy! Music's on!" W called out.

Upbeat pop music played, and assassins started snapping their fingers to the beat. They pulled out their daggers, arrows, and poles, creating a circle around me. Poppy clapped her hands, and tiki torches lit up around us. I braced myself and drew my knife. Kids came from every direction with long bamboo poles. I ducked, turned, and jumped away. One of the kids struck out with his pole, and I ran my

16

knife through it and slit it in half. I repeated the process for ten more assassins.

The assassins with the poles backed away, and next were my favorite: knives.

These assassins were more skilled and closer to my age. They came in close to my body. I blocked their slashes. I evaded their defense and touched their stomachs with my knife. This was the sign to back away since we were sparring, so when I stopped, the knife assassins stepped away.

Last were the hardest: the bows and arrows.

The arrows flew through the night sky, and I jumped to grab a shield that was hidden inside a tree in a little cardboard box that I cut through. Those shields were especially useful when Poppy felt like she needed to test an assassin.

Arrows flew, but the assassins who shot them dropped their bows. They turned their hands as though they were using steering wheels. These assassins were level threes who had already gotten their powers. They could control the arrows.

I flipped over most of the arrows. They missed me and stuck into the trees. The arrows I couldn't dodge were the ones I snatched from the air. I made it all look graceful, keeping the beat of the music with my movements.

J/K. The only person who could do that would be C. I, on the other hand, dove into the nearest bush until all the arrows passed overhead. I could hear Poppy telling the level threes to stand down.

Since I have a little time on my walk home, let me tell you a little bit about me and my relationship with ANW.

As soon as I held my first weapon, I fell in love with the art of combat. You might think I'm weird. That's what everybody thinks in school. I'm a freak, antisocial, whatever you call it. I am lonely. My parents are just like Clara's: busy and making money. Our parents started a business together.

So, the main reason people think I'm antisocial is because I never speak. I get tongue-tied. People just overwhelm me. Clara was the only one who came up to me in kindergarten, held out her hand and said, "Hi, I'm Clara, what's your name?"

This was my first real memory.

The second one was when I was around the same age. My babysitter had just put me to bed. My parents were out at a conference with Clara's dad. I wasn't sleepy at all. I climbed out my window and walked across the yard to Clara's house. Clara's mom wouldn't mind if I was there. She was the fun and quiet one, so I liked talking to her.

When I got there, Clara's mom was outside wearing a black leather dress. Her mask made of poppies sprayed around me, making me dizzy. I fell over and landed on the soft grass. She picked me up, scared that someone would see her, and ran over to a crowd of men nearby in the woods. This was where the level threes trained and hung out, before the big "golf tee building" was made. Of course, I didn't know that.

I saw them training and I wanted to join too.

"Me, me!" I squeaked.

Clara's mother laughed and said to the man next to her, "This young boy is a feisty one. When he is ready, we will train him."

As sure as her word, Clara's mom brought me to ANW the next night and gave me the black pants and shirt I had to wear, along with a wooden bow and arrow.

Since I didn't want to freak out my parents or my best friend, I didn't tell them about my secret. It's hard sneaking out at night, walking alone through the dark.

I got home around one in the morning. According to ANW, you *must* exercise after training, no matter how late it is. And if you don't, Poppy knows. Somehow.

I don't think Poppy wanted us to sleep. She had specifically mentioned that if you wanted sleep, and a normal life, you could go. You just needed to get mind-wiped.

Easy, right?

I tiptoed past my parents' bedroom and headed into a hidden door in my closet. When I was seven, my parents made this place so I can read comics and invite friends over.

Instead, this is where I keep everything related to ANW, from my first bow and arrow to my small knife and a blanket for when I want to crash on the floor, which is exactly what I did.

Forgetting everything else, including my ANW clothes, I fell asleep for about three hours. It was what my body was used to.

After waking up, I forced myself to get my lazy butt off the floor. I showered and put on some gym clothes and threw my ANW clothes into the laundry basket. I could clean up before my mom saw the mess. She wouldn't stir from bed until at least ten. I then crept down to the basement, where my dad exercised, which meant running for five minutes, getting a cramp, and watching Netflix until an hour passed. Then, he would spray water on himself and tell my mom he had exercised.

Parents.

I put on my ear buds and turned on my favorite song. I started the treadmill and had just started to run when my phone buzzed. I stopped running and nearly went flying. I turned off the treadmill and checked my phone.

It was a text from Clara. What the heck was she doing texting me at five in the morning?

Don't forget to meet me outside school today so we can talk about the Social Studies project. Sorry if this text woke you up. I couldn't sleep.

Oh no! The history project! I had forgotten all about it! If I remembered correctly, it was due today! I stopped working out and changed into some jeans and a shirt and tiptoed back into my room. Then, I ran over to my backpack and pulled out the paper with the project instructions. Next, I took out my computer and opened a Word document, but first I did my special ritual.

I went over to a little closet near the front door of my room and opened it. Inside, I had a stash of Twizzlers, M&Ms, and, the head honcho, KitKats. Whenever I'm feeling stressed or I start a big project, I eat something sweet to help me relax.

To get a sweet, though, you need a very special playing card, and this is no ordinary card. Every assassin gets a playing card when they reach level two, which scans their clothes and transports them. Mine has the seven of spades and my name engraved on one side, and on the other side, a red backing, just like regular cards. I made a lock so nobody could access my candy without my playing card.

After I had my candy, I sat down at my desk and tried to get some work done as the sun rose. Once I finished, I sat on my bed and watched the sunrise. As an alarm for seven beeped, I grabbed my cluttered backpack and a bagel from the kitchen and went to my parents' room. I hid my ANW clothes in the secret room, and promised myself I would clean it up after school.

My mom was still asleep. I gave her a kiss and tucked her in on the way out. My dad was outside and he took me to school in his car. "Have a great day!" he said when he dropped me off.

I waved, giving him a goofy smile.

Clara sent me a text saying she'd be late for school as usual. We would discuss the project after homeroom. Most people would think that with a hired driver to get you to school on time, you wouldn't ever be late. That doesn't apply to Clara. She's always late, and for no reason! One time she was late to homeroom and told our teacher she had to stop to complain about the meatballs they served for lunch.

Clara was given three detentions that week, while the rest of the class howled with laughter. That was the first day I actually saw her cry. It was at her house after she had served her first detention. When I asked her why she was crying, she said, "Damien, no matter how perfect you think my life is, it isn't. I try to be early and keep out of trouble for one reason. When I started kindergarten, my dad said only one thing: keep out of trouble. That's the only thing he expects from me, but I just had to go and open my big mouth." She sobbed.

"Don't worry," I said. "I'll just tell him that I got in trouble and you were covering for me. I'll say you took the blame for me."

"Really?" she asked, wiping her eyes.

"Always," I replied.

Clara gave me a big hug that day. I will never forget it as long as I live. What can I say? I'm a softie.

Remembering that, I stepped into the main hallway to slide down the railing in the stairwell, earning a glare from our principal, Mrs. Lafayette. I gave her what I called a blinding smile and went right past her.

Most of the kids near her frowned at me and whispered in close groups. I had just wanted to make Mrs. Lafayette smile, but instead, kids thought I was mean to her.

I slumped over. The only thing I wanted to do was not feel like an outcast, but that seemed nearly impossible, considering my record.

The second bell rang. I ran to my locker. Since my last name starts with an R, my locker is in the back. I looked around. There were no kids around, since everybody left for class before the third bell rang. That meant I had to hurry.

Suddenly, I heard a rustling sound. I turned around and pulled out my knife. I faced two men dressed in black, wearing a *very* familiar badge. The brown eagle with a black and white background explained everything.

"'Ello, Monsieur Richards," the man on the left said. The gold tooth in his mouth gleamed.

There was no point in calling out; the men had covered themselves in the dark purple powder that made them invisible.

"This is all we have to do? I should have gotten ice cream before," the tall man on the right whined.

"Shut up, you moron! We'll get ice cream *after* we finish the job," Gold Tooth yelled. The tall man nodded. "Okay, little prince, come here: we're not going to hurt you," Gold Tooth crooned.

"You think I'm *that* stupid? You two knuckleheads remind me of the burglars in *Home Alone*. Yep, you're like twins! I really wish I had a better match to deal with," I said.

Gold Tooth scowled and then smiled. He gave a nod to somebody behind me.

I groaned. "There's another one behind me, right?"

"Be careful what you wish for," a raspy voice croaked as he put a sleeping vital on my neck.

24

I had to keep myself from screaming in the hallways, as the hidden person behind me placed a small purple amulet on my neck, which I assumed was the vital.

The vital looks like an air freshener packet that you get at Bath and Body Works for your car, but this one had extra sticky tape, and a needle at the end that pricked my skin. The vital shut my body down. The lockers around me swirled. Gold Tooth's, the tall man's and the raspy man's faces blurred together.

The last thing I heard before my eyes closed was Clara saying, "Damien, where are you?"

CHAPTER 4

MEET THE MOST BORING
TEACHER OF THE YEAR

CLARA

I dashed through the school to make it to first period. I waved to Paulina, my best friend. She is only in two of my classes this year, but we still manage to hang out after school. We always make time hang out, even when we don't have classes together. It's been like that ever since I met her on a field trip in third grade. That was when she joined Ms. Fayman's class. She introduced herself and said she was from Saudi Arabia. Nobody wanted to get close to her even though she tried to make friends.

I saw that, and I felt really sad. New kids have the worst time making new friends, and I only know that because of how many new kids enter our school each year. They have to start their whole lives over again, and meet totally random strangers instead of their old friends.

Damien and I tried to ease the process of moving by making friends with the new kids. We did the same for Paulina. We sat with her on the class trip to the zoo. Ever since then, the three of us clicked.

Paulina and I scheduled playdates and sleepovers that didn't include Damien, though all three of us were close. There are some things only girls understand.

The bell rang and shook me out of my daydream. Mr. Tofu, my homeroom teacher, would joyfully hand out my 32nd tardy slip if I was late.

It's not like I wanted to hear his "*Young lady, you are in seventh grade now. I except more than this,*" speech. I just had a habit of running late even though San, my dad's driver, drops me off right at the early bell. I don't even do anything until the bell rings. I just sit around and daydream. Sometimes, I eat breakfast in the courtyard with my friends. We sit on a picnic blanket. Somehow, though, I'm late in the end.

I dashed to my locker and grabbed my books for the first three classes. Other than that, I did my daily ritual that included landing a small kiss on a photo of my mom and dad.

My mom is my go-to person for everything, and she always listens patiently until I'm done talking. Then she tells me what I needed to do. I love her to the moon and back. My dad is my cheerleader. He always cheers on the sidelines for anything I am doing. He shares my love of food, along with my sense of humor. I love him for that.

27

I took the shortcut past the nurse's office and landed in my seat just as Mr. Tofu (his real name, I'm not kidding) called my name.

"Clarissa Lemondola," he called out. He had a big smile on his puffy face as he started to write out a tardy slip. He was known for wearing the craziest suits—crazy in a bad way. One day, Mr. Tofu came in with PJ bottoms, a football jersey, and hiking boots. He blamed it on us. He said that since our book reports were so bad; he had fallen asleep while reading them!

Can you believe the nerve of this guy?

"Here, Mr. T," I said with a sweet smile.

Mr. T gasped and turned around. I pretended to be working.

He just shook his head and mumbled something under his breath. Guess my 32nd tardy slip would have to wait for another day.

I scanned the room for Damien. Normally, when Mr. Tofu lectures me on being late, Damien would do an imitation of him. No matter how miserable I feel, Damien knows how to cheer me up. Usually, that means putting a fart bomb or a whoopee cushion on Mr. Tofu's chair. That's one of the reasons he's my best friend. Not because of the pranks, but because he knows how to cheer me up.

I hate to say this, but there's only one person who can out-prank Damien, and that is the Black Fox. Damien rarely pranks at school, and kids hate it. To them, it is just a mess, and it wasn't even original. I refuse to believe that.

Everybody loves the Black Fox on the other hand. He was supposed to land a prank in school that day, like he said last week, but there was no sign of smoke, farts, or anything else that were Black Fox signature pranks. The only thing was, that the Black Fox was anonymous.

Anyways, Damien's desk was empty. He said he would be here that day. Maybe he just got sick the previous night, or maybe he finally convinced his parents he was sick by making fake vomit. He's tried that before and it *never* works.

"Damien Richards," Mr. Tofu called out.

"He's not here, Mr. T," I replied.

Mr. Tofu just shrugged and turned to the board. We were supposed to start the math problems before attendance. I waved at Sayre, who studies with me for classes.

"Where's Damien?" I whispered to Sayre.

Sayre shrugged her shoulders. Her bright her red hair bounced up and down. "I saw him annoying Mrs. Lafayette, but after that, it's like he disappeared."

Mr. Tofu cleared his throat. I got to work on the problems, although my mind was somewhere else. "Mr. T? Can I get a hall pass? Girl problems," I asked.

Mr. Tofu grumbled and scribbled a pass for me. I read it before I left. If I didn't get back in fifteen minutes, I would be in serious trouble. Game, set, and match goes to....Mr. Tofu. I stepped out the door and whispered, "Damien, where in the world are you?"

Maybe if he was hiding in a locker, which sometimes happens, or if he got lost, he would respond. No answer. I tried calling his name again and again. After that, I strolled around the empty school, hoping he was hiding in one of the classrooms. After ten minutes, I started to head back when I heard small footsteps.

I looked behind me to see Mr. Tofu's head. He smiled and pointed me to the principal's office. How does this guy hate my guts so much?

CHAPTER 5

I LISTEN TO THE WORST PLAN ON THE PLANET AND THEN REALIZE IT'S ACTUALLY GOOD

DAMIEN

"Where am I?" Ripping off the sleeping vital, I woke up to a bright light and a steel ceiling. One look told me everything I needed to know: I was trapped in a cage—an actual cage, a prison.

Around me, the room was painted a sickish yellow. If you repainted it and added some dots for sprinkles, it would have made a nice bedroom for a kid. Instead, it looked perfect for a criminal who wanted to interrogate his hostages. Blood was splattered everywhere. It made me want to throw up the cream cheese and bagel I had for breakfast.

Ohhhh, school. What am I going to do now?

My parents weren't that strict, except when it came to school. They had the biggest dream that their only child would be a successful doctor. Like *that* would ever happen now. My parents also never wanted me to miss school, even if I was sick. If I could stand up, not be contagious, and write a couple words, then I had to go to school.

Not that I minded going to school. I got to prank kids and teachers to my heart's content. They were my guinea pigs. If kids wanted to be mean to me and leave me out, then I had to do something to leave a mark at Holly Middle School. Whenever I prank, I'm anonymous as the Black Fox. The school praises the Black Fox for his notorious tricks. And not only my school. All of LA knows the Black Fox for his pranks. The pranks aren't harmful, but like I said, they bring joy to the people of Los Angeles.

Clara pranks on the side, but she's got so much on her plate, she'd only prank me once or twice a week. Pranking is my thing.

Speaking of pranking, I *was* going to leave a surprise today at school, but now maybe I will hold off pranking for a while. I wonder how I'm going to explain this when I get back.

If I get back.

Let's not think about that.

There was a single door near the front of the cage, but it had locks around every corner. Love locks, steel locks, locks with graffiti spray...There was even a Hello Kitty lock!

Basically, you name it, it was there.

There was only one person subhuman enough to put anyone in a cage.

"Skylock," I muttered under my breath.

General Skylock, the enemy of ANW. He's the leader of one of the biggest criminal empires. He has stolen over two billion dollars in cash. Clara's mom has been trying to catch him for five years, ever since he started, but she's had no luck. He's way too powerful. Skylock and his inhuman army have been wiping out assassin tribes everywhere. Yep, there are tribes everywhere.

Assassins like us live all around the world, some protecting, others raising chaos and doing what they like.

Our mission is to bring peace to the world by dealing with all the bad people. Basically, we're making the world a better place, but secretly. For some, making the world better means protecting people. For us, it means killing and catching the "You can't defeat me" people.

Get the idea?

Just then, Skylock came in as if he'd heard me say his name.

He sat down on a bucket and spat on the floor near me. He wore a leather jacket that had red and black stains. He wore a pair of beat-up sunglasses, and he sucked on a lollipop.

"Damien, just the boy I want to see," he sneered. He walked around me like a tiger about to devour its prey.

Nobody knows how Skylock came to be. Unlike all the psychopaths we've faced before, Skylock just started attacking assassins for no reason five years ago. The others at least had a reason for attacking, even though they weren't very good ones. Mostly you have the usual revenge. Once in a while, you have some crazy ones.

Skylock worked in the shadows, and rumor has it he was once an ANW assassin, but he became evil.

"For years I've *dreamt* that this day would come," Skylock said. I snorted. "What's so funny?" he snarled.

"Well, if your dream includes about 500 blood stains, a hundred-year-old jacket, and capturing the idiot of ANW, then it's here," I said, listing those things on my fingers.

"You idiot!" he growled. "You don't serve any purpose other than being the bait. Once your friends realize that their precious Damien Richards is being held in Skylock's arena, they'll walk right into my trap."

"By the way, how did you find me?"

"Smart one, aren't you?" Skylock scowled. "Let's just say I have some friends on the other side. They know when to bow down to me, and when to keep quiet."

He pulled a grubby black book out of his leather jacket labeled *Friendship Explained by Criminals to Criminals* by Ivanna B Krul.

I really wonder who was stupid enough to write that. You can't explain friendship. It just comes naturally.

I laughed. There was one little problem with his amazing plan. "There's no way they even know where I am."

Skylock pulled out his phone. He started to read out loud as he was typing.

"Dear Mrs. Rachel Lemondola, We have your friend's son. Surrender ANW or watch him die in two days. Signed, a friend," Skylock mocked. "Now, let's see the famous Clara Lemondola and her mother come and save you."

I jerked my head at that. "Clara? Why her? How do you even know her name?"

"You don't know?" Skylock said cautiously. "Well, if I recall, she is your worst enemy." He stopped, then smiled slyly. "And your best friend."

"What! I—I mean she would never be C, she's—Clara!"

"Well, I found this on the floor," he said. He held out a card. I gasped.

It was C's, or I should say, Clara's, badge. Like our playing cards, each assassin has their own badge. The badge has each assassin's real name on it. We aren't allowed to show it to anyone, but we always

35

have it with us. It's triangular and shows each assassin's name, birthday, address, and picture. It's like an ID for assassins, in case the police or another assassin tribe leader finds you.

As for Clara, I had never considered that my best friend would be an assassin. Sure, she has a hot temper and she doesn't have a lot of patience. But she's also my best friend, and I know her pretty well. Then again, I don't act quite like myself in ANW. I'm more ruthless and vicious as D than I ever would be as Damien.

I was in a state of shock and I forgot that Skylock was in the room. That only lasted a moment. He grinned. Seriously, he should go to a plastic surgeon to get his smile fixed if he plans on winning the Mister Global Evil pageant. Those pageants are very competitive, and usually include the most evil plans as the winning category. Face it, none of these guys are actually going to dress their best, even for a pageant.

As if he read my mind, his face turned beet red. He stammered and scowled at me.

"Done thinking about your last words? Your puny friends only have two days to save you. After that, say goodbye to ANW and to everyone you love!" Skylock cackled, throwing his hands up in the air. He swiveled around and left the room, leaving me in the dark.

Oh......great.

CHAPTER 6
MY PRINCIPAL TURNS INTO A HUMAN PRETZEL

CLARA

Mr. Tofu dragged me to the principal's office. Good thing the bell hadn't rung yet. I would be the laughingstock of the year if any kid saw me. I hung my head as I trudged along behind him. I only looked up when we arrived at the principal's office. The place is magical. The desk is the only piece of school furniture there, and it's draped in a white, chunky wool blanket.

At the far corner, there is a beanbag and hanging chairs. At the opposite end of the office, there is a floating pond. The pond isn't really floating, but it had been built to look like that, which is really cool. The ceiling lights were dimmed, and to replace the lighting, fairy lights were hung all over the place. The host of my favorite exercise channel, Phoe Ling, would fall in love the minute she saw this.

Right in the middle of all the serenity was my principal, Mrs. Angelica Lafayette. Mrs. Lafayette was the head honcho of Holly Middle, and she was proud of her history as a pageant winner. She wore turquoise yoga pants and a matching shirt. She was in a but-

37

terfly pose on top of a pastel mat. She chanted softly in an unknown language.

Mr. Tofu looked taken aback and turned away. He cleared his throat, and his face was bright red. Mrs. Lafayette stopped chanting when she saw us and smiled. "Rody! Clarissa! How nice of you to join us on yoga day! Come, take a seat. We can talk about why you decided to join me here while I do the tree pose. I have extra mats."

"Mrs. Lafayette, Clarissa is in trouble. She needs a consequence that is more serious than yoga." Mr. Tofu turned pale as Mrs. Lafayette twisted herself into a human pretzel.

"Oh dear, what is it now, Rody?" Mrs. Lafayette unbent and sat cross-legged.

"She used a hall pass and spent it looking for Damien Richards."

"How'd you know?" I said.

"Ms. Lemondola, you might recall that we have hallway security cameras here at Holly Middle, and Ms. Waterhouse was kind enough to remind me," Mr. Tofu replied.

I scowled.

Ms. Waterhouse, or Raina Waterhouse, is Holly Middle's mystery girl. Nobody knows anything about her, except that she's unpredictable. She challenged the student council to an arm wrestling

38

match, just so we could get black boots on the dress code.She ended up in detention two times a week. Nobody knows what to do with her, so they leave her alone.

But for some reason, she really enjoys getting me into trouble, even though I do nothing to her!

Mr. Tofu sneezed, and his hair flew off. Mrs. Lafayette gasped. Mr. Tofu was bald! His prized hair that he always bragged about was fake!

We looked away as Mr. Tofu slapped his hair back on. "Neither of you saw this, especially Ms. Lemondola, you understand? One word, Clarissa, and say goodbye to passing my class," Mr. Tofu said.

There were many good adult role models in my life. Mr. Rody Tofu was **not** one of them.

Mrs. Lafayette and I tried not to laugh. Then she stood up, trying to look very serious. "I will have a chat with Clarissa. Expect her by the end of the lesson," Mrs. Lafayette said.

Mr. T blew his nose and stormed out. The minute he left, Mrs. Lafayette and I laughed until we cried. After a couple minutes, she wiped a tear from her face.

"Now, what is the real problem?" she asked, bouncing up and down on a huge bouncy ball.

"Does Damien have an attendance record?" I said.

Mrs. Lafayette looked surprised, and then nodded. "Of course, Clarissa. But is that really the problem?" she asked, pulling out the attendance book. She flipped the book to R, then looked at Damien's record. Perfect attendance, except for today. "I think I see what you're getting at, Clarissa," she mused.

"Mrs. L? Is that okay if I call you that?"

"Of course, Clarissa."

"Do you mind calling me Clara? I prefer that over Clarissa. Every teacher calls me Clara, and I've tried to get Mr. T to say that, but he refuses."

"Of course, sweetheart. Now, for Damien's problem, tell me exactly how you interacted with him today." Mrs. L shut the book.

I told her everything, minus where I think he went. If I'm correct, then I'm going to have a long chat with my dear mom. And not a pleasant one. Mrs. L got very pale and fell off her bouncy ball. She doubled back onto the ball with a handspring. I gave a feeble clap. "Impressive handspring, Mrs. L, but everything okay?" I asked.

"Huh? Oh yes, everything's f..fine." Mrs. L seemed to be in a trance. She grabbed the phone and wrote a hall pass for me. She realized she was using a phone to write instead of a pen, and stopped.

She laughed and grabbed a pen. She scribbled the note and handed it to me.

"Here, use this to get back to class."

I was going to thank her, but before I could, the door shut, and I could see her grab her phone again and hurriedly talk to somebody. I bet it was either Damien's mom or my mom. Either one.

I left the room feeling dazed. If my principal was also worried, then something must be wrong.

I looked at the clock. It was almost 9. Class ended at 9:10, and I wanted a little time to talk to my friends, and not worry about being late to second period. I hurried to the classroom, where a frenzied Mr. Tofu was waiting, tapping his big foot.

"Ready, Ms. Lemondola?" he asked me.

CHAPTER 7
MRS. GARCIA DRAGS ME HOME
FROM HER SOAP OPERAS

CLARA

"**M**iss Lemondola, if you plan to use your hall pass to find Mr. Richards again, then I suggest you sit down. NOW," Mr. Tofu growled.

Everyone snickered. I covered my head and sighed. You see, middle schoolers can be explained in two sentences. One second, you can be their idol. The next? They humiliate you to idolize someone else. Unfortunately, this is a good description of at least 80% of the kids who go to my school.

This was going to be a bad morning. The bell rang, and all the kids ran out the door to greet their friends and make plans to meet between classes.

I grabbed a newspaper from Alvin Taylor, the Holly Middle School paper's editor-in-chief, who just happened to be in my homeroom. He was handing out the latest edition to whoever would buy it. "Nobody buying today? What's the headlines?" I asked. He looked super bummed out.

"The usual. Student Council is still fighting for equal teachers' pay, even though nobody's doing anything," Alvin replied.

"Ouch," I winced. "But shouldn't the teachers be fighting for their own rights?"

"The teachers gave up a long time ago, but students are still fighting because they haven't had any new supplies for the second and third graders next door." Quick note: Holly Elementary is right next door to us.

"That sucks. Is there anything I can do to help?"

"Just spread the word, that's all," Alvin said.

"Will do."

After class, I headed over to Madame Tuwa's French class. She is kind and sweet, but she's European. Don't get me wrong: I have nothing against people from Europe since I love it there, but they are nothing like Americans.

I've found that most people there are *very* honest, whether you like it or not, and if they like you, they like you.

Madame Tuwa is no different. Most kids really like her, and you hear praises from the eighth graders, or older high schoolers.

I especially like Madame Tuwa since she was my French tutor before she taught at the school. When the French teacher job opened, my parents recommended her to the school.

After plopping down my bag, I took a deep breath. I felt a bit bit better. Madame Tuwa's classroom is magical like most rooms in the school. She is known for interesting scents in the classroom.

Today, the scent of fresh bread wafted through room, and trust me, I know that scent personally, since my mom bakes bread. I really admire her for that. I mean, who has time to be an assassin, work a part-time job as a consultant, help her husband's booming business, and be a mom? She really is amazing.

Ugh, who am I kidding?

Even though I'm trying to be optimistic, I'm really worried about Damien for some reason. He *is* a prankster at heart, but this is a little extreme, even for him. His parents would be worried if he skipped school, so I'm pretty sure he's not out.

But where could he be?

Madame Tuwa interrupted my daydreaming/worrying and passed out work while she spoke.

"*Bonjour, mes enfants!* Today we will learn about French Architecture in the eighteenth century. Turn to page 52, and Bridget, start reading in French, please."

Bridget was a friend of mine in class. She gulped. Everybody knew she didn't have time to study for school. She had to help her mom at the animal clinic right after school and then drive an hour to see her dad. "Madame, I haven't studied. My dad was sick and I didn't have time to study. I got home at three a.m."

"So, you decide not to study for French, *oui*? Then you and the whole class will have extra French homework for the week." Like I said, Madame can be strict, but it didn't seem fair to not consider Bridget's late nights.

Bridget broke down and cried at her desk, and the rest of the class looked guilty. I went up to Madame Tuwa. "Madame, it is not fair to punish Bridget," I said in French. "My mother is friends with hers, and my mom was saying that Bridget was having a hard night since she had to stay with her dad in the hospital. He was in a car crash yesterday."

Madame Tuwa paled. "I'm sorry, *mon enfant,* I didn't know. But next time, tell me before class, *oui?*"

Bridget sniffled and nodded. She got up and hugged me. "Thanks, Clara. I owe you one."

"Any time, Bridget."

Maybe this day wasn't going to be so bad after all.

After French, I had Social Studies. We were focusing on how the U.S. came to be. The class went smoothly. While Ms. Summer droned on about the Civil War, I slept for an hour straight. When the bell rang, I headed straight for lunch. On the way, I met Paulina and we walked to the courtyard entrance.

"Where's Damien?" she asked, looking around.

"He's not here."

"Sick?"

"No, I honestly don't know. I'm going to ask Mom after school."

We entered the courtyard, but before I tell you about that, let me tell you how lunch usually goes. In the fall, we have a choice of picnicking in the courtyard or we can go inside the lunch hall. In the winter, we eat inside and then go outside. I decided to sit outside with my friends Aida, Bridget, and Paulina.

We sat down and Bridget talked about how she had found her brother singing in the kitchen in his boxer shorts, while she and her parents watched silently. The girls all howled with laughter, but I was too worried to join in. I sat quietly picking at the pasta my dad had packed. I loved my dad's ravioli, but I wasn't in the mood.

I picked up my phone and tried texting Damien, who always replies, no matter what time it is. My texts were marked *Read*, but there was no response. Damien is like a brother to me. I have been with him every day since we were toddlers.

Just as I finally started eating, an old woman walked toward me from the main building. It was crabby Mrs. Garcia from the front office. Her wrinkly dress from Walgreen's was stained with Coke. She always watched soap operas in the office. Quick head's up: She never, I repeat, never, comes out of the front office unless there is a serious problem. She turned her wrinkled face with sour lips covered with Cheeto dust toward me. This wasn't going to end well.

"Ms. Lemondola, your mother called. She says it is very urgent for you to come home."

This *definitely* wasn't going to end well.

47

CHAPTER 8
"VIP" SERVICE FROM A CRIMINAL.
THIS SHOULD BE GOOD.

DAMIEN

I peeked outside after trying every thing I could think of to get out. My bag was just outside the cage. The brown satchel laid forgotten and soaked.

I was feeling very hungry. I remembered that I had my watch, and I checked the time. Yes, a watch. Assassins aren't allowed to have phones on hand because it might cause a distraction. Call me old-fashioned, but I still wear a watch and don't look at my phone to tell the time.

Watch collecting is my dad's hobby. He has a watch from every country in the world except Morocco and Indonesia.

Anyway, it was 6:30. Ten hours since I had eaten. No wonder I felt so out of power. A normal human could survive without food for three days, but I'm pretty sure they wouldn't be able to move.

My mouth felt like sandpaper.

Thank God Poppy had taught us to hold food for a day, and I hadn't struggled too much with Gold Tooth and the other guy, so I could hold on for a few more hours.

After that, I'd be as good as dead. But let's not talk about that.

I reached into the pocket of my jeans and searched for my dagger. *They must have taken that too!* I sighed.

I hoped that I still had a few of the pranks that I had snuck into school today for the Black Fox, but Skylock had searched me to make sure I wouldn't be fooling around.

Touché, Skylock. *Touché.*

At that moment, Skylock came in whistling. He had the creepiest grin on his face, and he looked creepy without any expression.

"Don't worry, Damien. You won't find a weapon in a ten-mile radius," he said. Two of Skylock's goons brought in a throne and he sat down. Skylock's goons panted, sweat pouring from their heads.

He pretended to think. "You know what, Damien? I've reconsidered. Instead of starving you to death, maybe I'll let one of my fighters take you out quickly, even though you've probably been trained to hold food in for twelve hours," Skylock said.

Wait, I thought. *How would he know the exact amount of hours an ANW assassin can survive?* Poppy said each tribe had a different number of hours they could survive without food, depending on their training. *Unless....No, what am I even thinking? This guy couldn't be from ANW! We're too stealthy to be caught.* There was that traitor situation twenty years ago, but no ANW assassin has been caught since then.

I sighed. Well, after twenty years, they *had* to catch the idiot of ANW. So much for our perfect record. I had to go and mess it up.

I rolled my eyes. I really didn't have anything better to do, so I decided to rile up Skylock. I mean, what's the worst that could happen?

"Thanks, Skylock. I'm honored. Maybe a pussy cat would work just fine."

"Don't worry, Damien, just for you, I'll have my champion brought out. Just think of it like...a VIP service," Skylock smirked, wringing his hands as he spoke.

"So, where is this VIP service?" I laughed and air-quoted with my fingers.

Right, so I have had VIP service from numerous hotels, spas, and restaurants, but getting VIP service from a criminal is a BIG first. I wonder if they have monogrammed towels here. *Then* you know you're getting good service.

Skylock glared at me and pulled a lever beside his chair. The cage I was trapped in started rumbling, and it slowly dropped. The handle swung open. I peeked out the door of the cage. I checked if there were traps on the floor. Surprisingly, the floor, which was granite, was spotless. I cautiously stepped out.

The floor had sunk to become an arena. I knew what an arena was because I'd actually paid attention when Mrs. Leborn had covered the Romans, who are pretty cool, to be honest. They were way ahead of their time, just like the Egyptians. The one thing I didn't like, though, was that the Romans considered the number 13 unlucky. Now, I get why 13 was so unlucky. I just turned 13, and I was getting into a whole lot of bad trouble.

From above, Skylock yelled, "Let the games begin!" A crowd formed and _seating_ areas opened up. Seating areas. Can you believe it? All of Skylock's goons came and watched. I saw Gold Toothie and his ice-cream-loving pal take a seat right next to The Sleeper, who had a disturbing grin on his face.

"When's the show starting?" the ice cream man whined.

"Right after the commercials. Now, shut up," The Sleeper grunted. I turned the other way, and I saw what most of Skylock's goons' eyes were glued to. A commercial for shampoo played on the screen.

I watched it hoping it would stretch on for a while. Skylock, on the other hand, grew very bored. "I said, LET THE GAMES BE-GIN!" Skylock yelled even louder than before.

Skylock's associates turned the commercial off and pointed a camera directly at me.

A small gate opened and out came a huge tiger. It yawned. Its white fur moved up and down. It saw me and growled.

Did I mention I'm scared of tigers?

CHAPTER 9

MY BEST FRIEND'S AN ASSASSIN AND MY ENEMY. (WHAT COULD POSSIBLY GO WRONG?)

CLARA

I called San to pick me up. It was hard to keep my friends calm. It was even harder keeping myself calm. I had to promise them I'd call if something was wrong and to keep them updated.

The ten-minute car ride felt like an hour, and I had a really bad habit of kicking my seat. I got home to see my mom pacing up and down. She looked worried, which meant something was seriously wrong. I knew that my dad had gone to work, since his bag was gone. Usually my mom stayed home most afternoons. I helped her with chores and errands after school.

She saw me and finally took a break. She sat down. "Clara, do you know where Damien is?" she asked.

I shook my head. "No, I was wondering where he is. I think he's sick."

My mom shook her head. "Unfortunately, no. His mom called. She got a call from the school saying he wasn't at school today. He wasn't at home either," she said gravely.

"Ms. Lafayette got worried when I told her that Damien went missing—why?" I hoped she would overlook the fact that I just mentioned that I had been in the principal's office today.

"Wait, did you get sent to the principal's office? Why?" Moms who are assassins have a sixth sense for these things, I swear. I sighed. No point lying to my mom. After all, she gave birth to me.

"I—I faked a bathroom pass in Mr. Tofu's class because I was worried about Damien. I had a gut feeling. This wasn't a normal sick day or skipping class. Mr. Tofu spotted me looking for him, and took me straight to Mrs. Lafayette." My mom sighed, but then she smiled.

"I know that my girl doesn't get in trouble, and your gut feeling was right." Out of habit, I looked around for my dad before asking the question that had been troubling me the whole day. He doesn't know about ANW. I don't think he would approve if he learned that his wife and only child were assassins, even if we *are* the good guys.

"Do you think Skylock took him? Skylock threatened to take non-assassins to his palace if ANW didn't surrender."

"Now, why would you think that?" My mom's face clouded over.

I grimaced. "Let's just say I have a very, very, very *bad* gut feeling that Damien could have ended up there. Someone could have discovered my identity, and then captured Damien as ransom."

"I got a message from Damien's kidnapper. It was signed 'Your friend, Skylock.'" Of course. My stomach tied into knots. "That's not the only bad news. Skylock said he would only let Damien go if ANW surrendered."

"We got to go, but I have one more question."

"Go on."

"Why Damien? He could have taken anybody and made the trade. Why go the extra mile just to abduct my best friend?" There was a long pause.

"Honey, Damien is an assassin."

"But I've never seen him in training! I mean, he's been my friend since I was born."

"Believe it or not, Damien is D!" said Mom.

"No....he couldn't...Damien isn't that mean...besides, he would never kill me!"

"Remember when I taught you the rules of ANW?"

I nodded. The rules were easy. "One: Never reveal your identity. Two: Don't act like yourself. Act like a new person."

My mother stopped me, and I realized why. The mask was only part of the disguise. For other people to not recognize me I had to turn away from my soft side and become the demon inside me. I realized that Damien must have done the same thing. No wonder we didn't get along. "Now you know what he had to do. Damien also turned away from his soft side and became hard and prickly. Say the next rule."

"Three: To survive, making friends is not advised. Empathy could kill you."

Even though I knew why Damien wasn't at school, I was still confused. "What should I do now? I...I don't even have my code-name, not to mention powers!"

"Just go get dressed."

I walked up to my room and shut the door behind me. I reached into the breast pocket of my denim jacket and pulled out a four of hearts card.

After a quick eye scan, the card turned into a mini tablet. This is how assassins change their clothes and contact others quickly in case of emergency. You also have to carry clothes in case something happens to your card. Since the card is loud (and annoying) you can't change in any public place where your enemies might be around, such as a public bathroom, or anywhere, honestly. You have seven options: a rebel suit, which consisted of a black top and black leggings (black shirt and shorts for boys, which they didn't like very much); a stealth suit tailored for the assassin's liking (for both genders); your formal outfit, which contains a cream-colored ballgown and black tuxedo for boys; every disguise ever made; another pair of regular clothes; and ANW's uniform, which for girls contains a spaghetti-strap dress and for boys, a black shirt with pants. I personally don't like the dress since it's too long, and I'm not allowed to cut it, but if you want to be in ANW, you have to have the dress. Hopefully after I reach level three, maybe I can switch it out for something else.

The dresses and other required clothing are negotiable, as long as you talk with my mom first.

I stood back, and the tablet scanned my body. The dress with spaghetti straps appeared on me. I felt a cool wind tickle my eyes. I brushed my hair into a long ponytail, put on my mask, pulled on some fingerless gloves, and grabbed some combat boots. I sat on the bed and clutched my necklace. It was a gift from my mother for my sixth birthday. In ANW, your necklace is a key for your level three ceremony. Literally! The jewelry looked like a gold key, with diamonds studded across the top part. The kids say that a door opens for you when you prove your loyalty to ANW.

I tucked the necklace into my dress.

In a messenger bag, I put a knife, some harmless pranks, a change of clothes, and some food. It was too risky to carry my phone. Our enemies could hack into our phones, but I needed mine in case Damien was able to text. Just for this time, I took it with me.

I grabbed my mask and threw it on. The mask stuck. I stared at myself in the mirror and dashed out.

Great-great-great-great gran Giovanna had designed my mask herself. It had silver swirls and an "ANW" logo stamp.

I headed to the kitchen. My mom was there. She was dressed for ANW, too. "First things first, are you sure do want to do this?" she asked.

"Definitely. There's no going back."

She looked frightened for a minute. She cleared her throat when she saw me looking at her.

"Here's the address." She handed me a stained piece of paper.

"Oh, and yes, Clara, I have excused you and Damien from school."

"But how did you manage to excuse Damien?"

She told me that she spoke to Damien's mom and convinced her that she was taking Damien and me to a press conference in Switzerland. It would be a huge learning experience.

"How *exactly* did you do *that* without mentioning ANW?"

"Let's just say I had a little help from Hypno." She pulled out a huge basket from a kitchen cabinet and opened the fridge.

Hypno is my mom's secret weapon, the mind-wiper I talked about earlier. Now, I wonder what else that weapon can do. "Here's a basket of supplies and food for the three of you." My mom set the basket on the table.

"What do you mean by the three of us?"

"Since you're underage, and you are the number-one teen wanted by our enemies, I'm sending you with two other assassins. Their codenames are A and R. I'm guessing they're about your age." She opened the garage, and the door hummed.

I was shocked. My mom wanted me to save Damien from the world's most powerful criminal with two strangers? I made up my mind. I would try to convince her that I should level up earlier.

"Mom?"

"Mmm?" She unlocked the car and adjusted the seat.

"Why can't I level up earlier?"

"Well, because it's a rule."

"Why, though?"

"Well, not after..." She drifted off. "Because I made the rule. Don't ask your mother why." Apparently, my mom didn't share my confusion. She whistled as she packed the basket in the back of our car. She motioned for me to get in.

It was too dangerous to have San drive us. If somebody saw us, it could blow our cover. It would also be odd if I just walked into ANW. ANW's leader is supposed to be very mysterious. Poppy comes and goes as she pleases. But nobody knows I'm related to ANW's leader except a few people. We can't be seen together.

I slid into my mom's BMW. Just then, my phone beeped. It was Paulina. *Hey girl! Thought we were meeting up for a study session after school.*

I texted back. *Hey P! Can't. Family business. TTYL!*

The other girls had sent similar messages, minus the study session. It was nice that people cared about me, but it was time to focus. I shut my phone off and put it in the front seat pocket. I didn't want the whole mission to go *kaboom* because of my phone. Nevertheless, I was in for a surprise, and it was not good.

CHAPTER 10

WHAT'S WORSE THAN GOING ON YOUR FIRST MISSION WITH TWO STRANGERS? POSSIBLY NOTHING.

CLARA

When I got to ANW, my mom parked near a large oak tree and hid the car under a tarp. We walked into a secret door that was cut into the leader's tent to get to the middle of ANW grounds. My mom greeted the group of women she works with. Their codenames are Ringer, Lab, and Dollface.

They all wore the same black-lace, spiderweb-covered dress. Each one had a different symbol on the right side of the dress. Ringer wore a bell, Lab wore a puppy, and Dollface had a doll's head. Their codenames match their powers perfectly.

Ringer is Black and has a large afro. She also has a very big heart. She has the power to amplify sound. Ringer joined ANW when she was five, just like me. She is a very good friend of my mom's, and one of the people I really trust. I know her identity. It's Ringer in ANW, and Seana Dymaod when we're in public. She is in charge of amplifying the announcements at ANW.

Lab, or Marlena Fase, can do everything a dog does, except turn into one. Marlena met my mom in Hawaii when they were on vacation as kids. Later, when they were around fifteen, my mom wanted Marlena to join ANW. My grandma made a special card for her so she could come and go from Hawaii to California. My mom said that when Lab got her powers, they malfunctioned, so she had all the characteristics of a dog. One of her powers is the infamous force-field she can create, like a dog protecting a herd of sheep.

Dollface, on the other hand, doesn't share her name with me, only my mom. I'm fine with that. She's more than just a pretty face. Even though she has the pretty blond hair and blue eyes, don't let that fool you. She is a genius. She was once in a Miss Diamond pageant, where she was a victim of a manipulative contestant. The contestant wanted to get rid of her, who was the reigning champion. Before my mom dealt with the threat, Dollface finished the job. By the time the police and my mom (who was undercover) showed up, Dollface had the contestant strapped to a chair. Even today I have no idea what she did that was so scary that made the contestant beg for the police to show up. My mom invited her to join ANW, and she agreed. She was also one of the few assassins who requested not to have any powers, and she doesn't need any. My mom told me she has a black belt in karate and had been a boxer as a teenager. I wouldn't be surprised if she was a neurosurgeon or a scientist who finds a cure for cancer in the real world.

The three ladies smiled at me. It was only fair that they knew I was Poppy's daughter, since they were among the few who knew my mom's identity.

"Where are the level twos?" my mom asked Lab.

"In the combat circle. They're fooling around waiting for you."

I smiled. Now *that* sounded much better. I started to run over, but my mom caught me by my dress. "Not tonight, my poisonous spider. We have work to do," she said.

I grumbled. Just then, my mom's tent door opened. A boy with a black t-shirt and pants and a girl with a black leather stealth suit entered. My mom introduced me to the two teenagers. The girl was R and the boy was A. They didn't have their codenames yet.

"Hey," R said.

"Hi C, it's nice to be working with you," A said. I guess he was trying not to get on my bad side, like most assassins.

"Thanks, you too," I said. "I guess we better get going."

"Correct, C. If you three have anything to say, contact me on your card," my mom said. I have to remember to call her by her codename though.

"How will we get to Skylock's palace?" A asked.

My mom replied, "Since you know that it's dangerous to be in a car when you are with ANW, I'm afraid you will have to walk. I think it's a day's journey. I can't come with you. I have to defend ANW headquarters from Skylock. C already has the address. Judging by her face, I think she already knows exactly where the palace is."

I nodded. Skylock's palace was familiar, because surprisingly, my mom and I had visited five years ago, when it was a monument and before it had conveniently been closed. Now I knew why.

Car rides are magnets for assassins. If any enemies know you're in a car while you're with ANW, they come running. It's like an all-you-can-eat buffet for anybody who wants to destroy ANW.

I shrugged. "Fair enough." Walking wasn't too bad.

We got ready. My mom handed us the basket of food and water. We set off as the sun set. We walked into the woods avoiding the main roads. It was the worst time for an assassin to be out, but who knew what Skylock was going to do with Damien?

CHAPTER 11

I OFFEND A VICIOUS TIGER

DAMIEN

Why did it have to be tigers? Why not a horror clown or a spider queen? Anything else! This kitty cat can do more damage than C's dagger, and trust me, that can shed a lot of blood.

Tigers paralyze me. Already I could feel my bones slowly turning to stone, and my legs falling asleep. My heart beat a lot faster than normal. Was that sweat on my lip?

If you're wondering why an assassin is afraid of a Siberian tiger and not afraid of anything else, let me tell you. My mom had this great idea to take me to the zoo for my fourth birthday. A new tiger had just come into the zoo. They had built a new habitat with a glass walkway, so people could see the tiger underneath. We went there the first day it opened, and the zoo staff didn't have the brains to test it first. I was the first person to step onto the walkway. It crashed and I fell into the tiger's lair.

If it wasn't for my quick thinking (as a four-year-old), I wouldn't have made it.

No, not really.

I picked up a branch and held it like a sword, like the heroes I'd seen on Disney Jr. The hungry tiger ignored the stick and lunged at me. So much for my survival skills.

Quick note: I hadn't found out about ANW yet.

I would have been dead meat if my mom hadn't jumped down and grabbed me. We crashed through the outer glass of the exhibit. The tiger clawed my shoulder and left a deep scar. Only my parents know about it. It's nasty. It is a reminder to this day to stay away from tigers, even stuffed ones.

Oh, and if you're wondering what happened to the tiger, well, let's just say, it found a better home in the wild. I'm glad it got reunited with its family and wasn't left alone.

We, on the other hand, sued the zoo. The zoo had kidnapped all the animals for its exhibits . The zoo shut down, and all 306 species of animals were returned to their homes safe and sound .

Our school went on a trip to the animal habitat last year, which is different from a zoo. There, instead of animals in cages, you find happy animal families in pens. The habitat includes rescued endangered species. There, they are cared for to increase their population. Before I went, my parents swore there weren't any tigers, that I would be perfectly safe. They didn't realize that a tiger family was being shown that day. You can guess what happened.

Spoiler: It included three fire alarms, screaming twelve-year-olds, and a pair of sunglasses.

I realized something after remembering all the horrific episodes I've had with tigers: I didn't have anything to fight the tiger with.

"Skylock!" I yelled. "You really wouldn't let an assassin fight an animal without a weapon, would you?"

The crowd went silent. They all looked at Skylock. Not letting a prisoner fight fairly was a disgrace, even for a criminal.

What? We live in the 21st century. So, criminals have rules these days. It's sort of like when my parents were little, seatbelts weren't needed. Today, if I take off my seatbelt even for a second, the police will stop our car and give my parents a ticket.

"You've beat me at your own game, Damien," Skylock grimaced and motioned to one of his associates to toss me a dagger. I swirled around, gripping the dagger until my knuckles were white. The tiger swiped a claw at me. I ducked and turned around. I poked the tiger's tail with my dagger.

"Hi, kitty cat," I teased the tiger.

The tiger swiped at me. Skylock sat back, looking angry.

"Huh, I expected something more than rotten comebacks from one of ANW's top assassins," Skylock yelled. The crowd roared.

"Really? I'm flattered," I shot back. "Again, you got the wrong person, Skylock. It's not me, it's Clara."

"You're right!" Skylock gushed like a three-year-old. "She's falling right into my trap. Just about now, she should encounter my best executioners.

Uh-oh. That's not good. Even for somebody like Clara, executioners are hard. They're faster, smarter, and quicker than any assassin, if trained properly. Don't ask me to describe them, 'cause I won't. I could explain a lot of things, but nowhere is the word *executioners* touching my mouth.

"First of all, Clara's not stupid. She won't walk into your trap, Skylock!" I yelled. "Secondly, she can fight her way out. We will stop you." At least, I hope so. Or else, I'm never getting out of here.

CHAPTER 12
WATCHING SCI-FI MOVIES SAVED MY LIFE

DAMIEN

I lunged at the tiger. It growled so ferociously that Skylock jumped out of his chair and fell into the arena and landed near me. His sunglasses flew off his face and broke near him.

How is this guy a criminal mastermind?

I peered into his face. He reminded me of somebody I'd met before. Someone I knew very well. Then, it hit me. No, no it couldn't be her. The girl I know best—Clarissa Lemondola, the most loyal, honest, and caring person I knew. My best friend.

Something in my gut told me he was related to Clara somehow. Maybe it was the way he moved, or the way he talked. I helped Skylock up; he looked bewildered.

"Who...who are you? Where am I?" Skylock said. His face turned white.

"The question is, who are you?" Immediately, his face changed again, he was angry.

"Get off me, boy!" he cried, shoving me to the floor.

My gut and my knowledge of sci-fi movies told me one thing: I had to figure out and reverse Skylock from whatever spell he was under before he killed me.

"Do you know Clara? Ummm....Clarissa Lemondola?" I asked him gently. It wouldn't hurt to try. What if Skylock knew Clara as somebody other than an assassin?

It was worth a try. Meanwhile, the tiger seemed intrigued by the conversation. It stayed close to me but didn't attack.

Skylock's face turned paler and kinder again.

"Clarissa? Rachel's second-grader, right? Yes, she's my niece, the darling thing."

My face fell. This man, apparently Clara's uncle, saw her last when we were 8 or 9. If I recall, Clara had mentioned that her parents were both only children, so who was this?

"Uh, sir—" I started.

"I don't know who you are, but a mysterious man in a cape and hat brainwashed me. The only way to change me back is by reminding me of my past. You did it, my boy," Skylock said.

I stopped to think for a second and the tiger roared, ready to finish the fight. He must have sensed the drama was over.

"Sir, stand back for a minute. I need to finish this beast off." I positioned myself, ready to kill the tiger.

"No, don't! He's my pet, Fluffy. I'll find a piece of meat," Skylock said.

Who the heck would name their tiger Fluffy? But if you're a criminal mastermind, it really doesn't matter *what* you name your pet.

When Skylock came back, he fed the tiger a piece of meat and it fell asleep.

"What's your name, young man?" Skylock asked me.

"Damien," I replied.

"You're Damien, the boy who is friends with my niece. You and her were always inseparable, so I guess I met you when I used to visit with Clara. But are you really *that* Damien? But that couldn't be— you should be a second-grader."

"Sir, umm, how do I put this? It's been five years since you've been Skylock. Your niece, Clara, is now almost thirteen."

"Well, that makes more sense. By the way, how *did* you end up here in this palace?"

"Before we start, um, if you don't mind me asking..." I started. "I'm pretty sure Skylock is not your name."

Skylock laughed weakly. "No, my dear boy, my name is Arthur Wells."

"So, Arthur. You—well, Skylock-you—kidnapped me. That's how I got here. Don't you remember?"

"Unfortunately, no. You need to fill me in."

"Hold up. I think I have some lunch left in my backpack, so let's share it, and I can catch you up on the last five years of the world."

"How do you know you can trust me?"

"What?" I asked, startled.

"How do you know you can trust me? I could turn evil at any moment," Arthur replied.

"Trust is a strong word these days, Arthur, but I have faith that you're good. Shall I tell you about the world now?"

"You may, Damien," Arthur smiled.

I told him about how much the world had changed. He wanted to know more about Clara, so I told him everything I possibly could. He listened eagerly, and I felt really bad for him. This man missed five years of his life.

"Well, I'm going to do everything I can to get us out of here," I said after finishing my tale. Arthur winced. "There is something you're not telling me, right?"

"Noooo...." Arthur squeaked and then sighed. He threw his hands up in the air. "Yes, Damien. Once somebody frees me, the executioners have permission to kill me *and* the person saving me. In that case, you."

CHAPTER 13
I TRY TO MAKE FRIENDS WITH ASSASSINS, AND IT DOESN'T GO TOO WELL

CLARA

"So, how did you end up in ANW?" I asked R and A. We were deep in the forest, and for about an hour, we walked in silence. I wasn't used to that, so I tried to make small talk.

"Well, I just got in and they asked me if I wanted to kill, duh," R shot back, rolling her eyes.

So much for that.

"R, be nice. Sorry, she's just adjusting to this whole assassin thing. We recently joined, and she's not having an enjoyable time," A apologized. "It's a really nice experience, and I really like it here. We'll just make the most of it."

I admired A's positivity. For some reason, it seemed familiar. I shook it off, trying to stop my head from coming to weird conclusions. "Oh, it's fine. I know the feeling," I lied trying to relate to the girl.

"No, you don't," R shot back.

My temper was rising. This girl knew how to bring out my bad side. Usually, I don't raise my temper at all, but there are some exceptions. A memory played back in my head. I was only five, and had just started kindergarten. I would yell at everybody, even the teacher. My behavior chart was filled with red dots, and I was in time-out most of the time. My parents didn't know what to do with me, but they somehow got me to calm down by meditating. My mom took me to ANW at night. I never told anybody about it, and even though Damien knew, he never said a word.

"I joined a year ago, along with R," A said. "Last Halloween, she and I were hiding behind a shop, and we saw one ANW associate without his mask on. I think his name was D."

_La-di-da._ What a surprise.

"Well, then, why didn't D wipe your memory? It's protocol," I asked A.

"He didn't want to, so he brought us to Poppy," A replied. "She recruited us on the spot."

I shrugged. Makes sense. Damien would never wipe anybody's memory, especially if he thought they would be beneficial to ANW. _Oh, boy. Better stop thinking about him, or I don't think I'm even going to make it to tonight._

"C, there's something weird going on." A's voice brought me back to my senses.

I heard rustling in the bushes. I silently motioned for R and A to stop, and then took out my dagger. R pulled out a spear. A grabbed his bow and nocked an arrow. We circled around. Suddenly, an executioner sprang from the bushes.

Hold on, maybe I should clear that up. Sure, I said I can't tell you everything about ANW, but you need to understand this nuisance.

The difference between assassins and executioners is that executioners are plain evil and work for Skylock. Their badges said it all: they were from Skylock's palace. The badges are black and white with a big brown eagle on them. Skylock knew what was going on. They were here for one reason. To kill us.

CHAPTER 14

WE FIGHT AND LOSE...OUR FOOD

CLARA

I pounced on the executioners, or execs, as we called them in ANW. They are almost impossible to defeat because they learn your fighting technique. They can mimic your skills and then kill you. In short, you have to defeat them in less than ten minutes. I counted five execs. I could not let even one of them out of my sight, or Skylock would know we were coming for him.

My leg went flying and knocked an exec in the head. Two flew from both sides. I jumped up and they knocked heads. I snickered. That's one of my favorite (and most enjoyable) moves my mom taught me.

A and R took on the other two together. A tossed his bow in the air and dove under one of the exec's legs. A slid under. He grabbed his falling bow. He briefly poked a poisonous arrow into the exec's leg. The exec fell to the floor. R jumped over the knocked-out exec and kicked him in the face.

My mother made it very clear that we were not to kill anyone unless it was critical. As she said, "We're assassins, not execs." Knocking somebody out is okay, especially if they are an exec.

We all sat down. It was nearly noon, and we had to rest. When we looked for our food, we couldn't find it. A admitted that he'd thrown the food to the side during the fight. R smacked a hand to her forehead. "Is there something you can do without messing up, A?"

"Let's not fight," I said hastily. A fight was the last thing we needed. I decided we would keep walking until we got some food. We kept on until the sun set. We could only see part of the sun through the tall oak trees. The forest seemed never-ending. I was getting sick of seeing trees. I had a huge headache.

I tried to find some food, but there were only bushes and trees nearby. My headache was getting dangerously strong. I felt really dizzy. My stomach grumbled loudly. I was hungry, and if I didn't get food soon, I was going to collapse.

Beside me, A nearly fainted from exhaustion, and R kept dozing off as she walked. She kept swinging her sword really close to my face accidentally.

I fell to the ground. I couldn't get up. My eyes flickered, but I fought the urge to sleep. I couldn't give up, not now. We were so close to Skylock's palace.

I saw R and A changing into normal clothes and pulling off their masks. Their faces were blurry through my half-closed eyes. I shut my eyes and listened to what they were doing. I felt R and A dragging me by the arms. I saw light through my closed eyes. oThey said "Hold on, Clara," and "You're almost there."

I opened my eyes for a couple seconds. I could see that we had exited the woods. Now we were on a strip of pavement near a solitary house. R and A looked like they were running to that house. I struggled to keep my eyes open. As they ran back, I blacked out.

79

CHAPTER 15

BOY TALK

DAMIEN

"Really? You're just telling me now?" I groaned. Arthur picked his fingernails and looked at the ground.

"Well, there is one thing we can do," Arthur said. "In the front of the palace, there is a map room guarded by two execs. If we can get past them, that's where all the weapons and maps are so we can find a...less painful way to get out. We might have to wait a bit, though. I'm pretty sure we both need some rest."

I nodded. That seemed fair. I was numb everywhere, and Arthur had a huge bruise on the side of his head.

"Do you have any clothing in your bag?" he asked, staring in disgust at his leather jacket. He threw off the jacket, and lowered his sunglasses. Then I gave him a stray brush and an old scarf I had in my backpack. He combed his hair, which made him look more a regular person, not the guy who terrorized the whole world of assassins in one go.

"That's more like it," I told Arthur, and he smiled.

"I'm guessing I owe you an explanation," he acknowledged.

I nodded. There's no way Arthur just walked in and got brainwashed. "I met Clara's Aunt Ariana when I was twenty-five living in Hong Kong. We got married and moved here three years later. Then, she told me about her sister, Rachel. Ariana knew her sister lived in California, and when she saw an ad with Clara in it, Ariana sent *me* to talk to Clara's father since Ariana wouldn't go. She still thought Rachel was mad at her. Fortunately, Rachel was in the office that day. When I introduced myself, Rachel told me to meet her at ANW, and that's when I met you two."

"Hold up. How do *you* know about ANW?" I literally screamed, shocked.

"Whoops, I might have not mentioned that part to you, sorry." Arthur shrugged. "I joined ANW after Ariana left. I was just a little older than you. At that point, Rachel, er, Poppy, was just getting used to being leader. I met Clara's aunt because I *was* in ANW, and I was part of the group sent out to hunt her down, and bring ANW's traitor to Poppy." Arthur squirmed. " As you can see, things didn't work out that way. I ran away from ANW. Moving on. I kept visiting you two until five years ago. I had just gotten off work, and I was running home when I got ambushed by two men in black. It was the Shadow Man and his assistant, The Sleeper."

"Wait, you said you visited us until five years ago. When we were eight. Why didn't I see you?" I said.

"Damien, I was an assassin, too, remember? Rachel, Clara's mom, reminded me that I had to be careful when I visited you and Clara. Apparently, you were two of the top assassins in ANW, and could crack almost any riddle, even ones that stumped level threes. You both would immediately figure out who I was if I seemed suspicious in the least part," Arthur explained, but I quickly intervened.

"*Why* didn't Poppy want Clara to see you and Ariana?"

"Like you said earlier, trust is powerful, especially between sisters. Takes a lot of time to make trust, and a second to break it. Ariana never told me what she did to betray ANW, but I let her take her time and come clean when she wanted to, not when I wanted her to. To avoid being detected by you two, but not to feel like I was stalking you, I disguised myself. Do you remember the man who gave the level one classes every once in a while, before he was fired by Poppy?"

A lightbulb went on in my head. "Ohh, you mean the guy who always had a scar like a lightning bolt? I loved his classes! But, what does that have to you with you?" I asked.

Arthur pushed back his hair, and revealed a lightning bolt scar. I gasped. "I guess you know the rest, right?"

I nodded. "You got kidnapped and knocked out by the raspy man, which I think is the Sleeper based on what you said, right?"

"Well, yes. So The Sleeper knocked me out, and took me to his personal lair. I was one of the Shadow Man's brainwashed minions. Eventually, people thought I was the bad guy and the rest is history."

I went over and hugged him. "It doesn't matter who you were. Life gives you second chances. It matters if you take them."

"Wow. Are you Dr. Phil?"

We both cracked up. "Something like that," I replied. "I'm ready to go."

He nodded. "So am I. But there's one more thing. The door outside us has thirty execs, all armed with the most powerful weapons ever, so we're going to have to think of a plan before we set out."

CHAPTER 16

I MEET...MY AUNT

CLARA

"C.....C!"

I woke up at once and tried to get up. A and R had their masks back on, and they looked around anxiously. Next to R, there was a woman who I recognized as the traitor ANW banished. My mom had shown me her face as soon as I joined ANW. That was a memory I will never forgot.

My mom had told me about a woman who left ANW for RAID twenty-five years earlier. RAID was the largest criminal group at the time. She told them all about ANW. My grandmother stopped her just before the she told RAID where the ANW headquarters was located. I sprang up, but R and A held me down. They knew what I was thinking. What was I doing here? I gave them a menacing glare.

"C, she saved your life," A replied calmly. "She carried you into the house, and then fed you some soup.

"You were out for a good hour or more," R said.

Even though he was right, I still didn't want to believe A. The woman smiled sadly at me, as if she wanted to say something.

R and A propped me up to sitting. The woman said she wanted to have a word alone with me. R and A went out, and I sat in one of the chairs near the bed.

"I am Ariana Velez. As your mother might have told you, I was an ANW associate, but a foolish one. Your mother and I fought bravely side-by-side."

"How do you know me?" I asked. Ariana handed me a mug of hot chocolate and continued. She looked really guilty.

"When I was in ANW, I developed a spray that could remove even the most stubborn masks, especially ones that were crafted with magic hands. It doesn't matter now, since the minute you take me back to ANW, I'll be memory-wiped," she said.

Hmm, a spray to remove masks. Obviously, after I take this woman back to ANW, I really need to get my hands on that spray.

Also, she was right about the magic hands. My great-grandma Giovanni made my mask.She had the power of making really powerful objects, such as this super-sticky mask.

Ariana stopped there, which meant I had to say something. I saw her more clearly now. She looked like she was in her thirties. She had a mischievous smile. Her hair was blood-red and cut into a bob,

She wore a white-lace cardigan, an aqua shirt, and a pink circle skirt. She looked uncomfortable. Her face turned sickish.

She had pale skin like my mother. She had blue eyes that looked like a fire burned in them. Just like mine.

"How did you know my mom?" I asked.

"She's my sister," she confessed.

CLARA

"No, you're...you're my mom's sister?" I fell back into the chair, shocked. "You're my...aunt? But that can't be. Mom never said she had any siblings!"

"She was wrong," my aunt replied. "Here's why. Before I begin, I want you to touch my card and hold my hand."

"Hold on. How do I even know I can trust you?" I tried to look intimidating. "You ran away from ANW, handed yourself willingly to RAID, and worst of all, you betrayed your sister's trust. My *mom's* trust." I sounded really mean, but I couldn't sugarcoat the truth. My whole life, I've been missing a part of my family. Now I intended to get it back.

"Ask me something about your mother that only you would know," my aunt replied.

I thought for a second. My mom was shockingly open with the stuff she *could* share in her life. Then it dawned on me. "What was Rachel Charity Lemondola's prophecy dream?" I asked my aunt.

Now, we should get to explaining what a prophecy dream is, right? A prophecy dream is necessary if you ever want to be the next ANW leader. Think of it like the confirmation email you get when you buy plane tickets. My mom said she only shared her prophecy dream with three people. She told my grandma and me. I always wondered who the third person was, but now I know. In a prophecy dream, you dream about a future scenario that will happen in your life.

"Rachel dreamed she would give up her spot at the pageant near our vacation house in Hawaii when she was twelve and a half," Ariana said. "Does that answer your question?"

"Fine for now. But when we get back Damien, I want the past in full detail," I said.

"Actually, before you interrupted me, I *was* going to use the card to show you as much of the past as I could. The rest I will explain to you *and* your mother in full detail. I promise."

An old ANW playing card that looked like mine was in my aunt's hand. The card looked like it was on its last leg. "This card was deactivated, but I fixed it so I could access the last memory I have of ANW."

88

As soon as I touched the card, my eyes shut. I felt like my soul was falling through a never-ending chute. When I opened my eyes, I really was falling through a black void.

My aunt stood next to me.

"This is normal," she said. "It'll be over soon."

The falling stopped after a couple seconds, and I landed on a black sofa facing a huge TV. My aunt turned on the TV, and I saw a sandy beach on the screen.

I saw two girls around my age playing in the ocean. A boy stood with them laughing. He looked like my dad. No, scratch that. I think it was my dad, *waaaay* before they got married. They all played together, splashing each other in the ocean. They came out dripping with sea water.

A woman, who I thought was my grandma, scolded the girls. They looked like my mom and aunt, but the first girl had blond hair and the second had black hair. My grandma sent my father home.

I rubbed my eyes to find my grandma dressed in her ANW uniform. My aunt and mom were dressed the same way. Grandma scurried them into a car and drove north. They got out of the car after twenty minutes. My grandma looked around and pushed the girls through a bush.

On the other side, there were three cards face-up on three slabs of rock.

They all used the same card to get in, I thought, surprised.

"Rachel, Ariana, please hold up the card and look directly at it," said my grandma.

The three completed the process. Grandma pulled a lever and they descended to the secret ANW meeting place underground. "Welcome, my fellow esteems," my grandma said in six languages. I understood all of them; learning languages was part of our training. "Today, two more ANW kids become adults by performing the sacred ceremony. Let us begin," she said.

I looked away. I knew I wasn't allowed to look. My aunt took my hand and said, "Clarissa—"

"Clara, please."

"Clara, this is the outdated version of the ceremony. There was no high-featured stuff in those days. And it was all done in one day. Don't worry, this is not the actual ceremony that you will be doing."

I felt relieved. First, the girls sat in a sauna, where they purified themselves. Then, cleaned and dressed, my aunt and mother transformed their facial features. My mother's eyes went from deep cherry red to aqua blue; her hair changed from a lemon-drop color to raven black. Now she wore a golden dress with a sweetheart cut, something the little ones weren't allowed to wear, including me. The dress had embroidered poppies and sequined vines, trailing to the bottom of her knee-length hem.

I snapped my fingers. The dress was familiar. It was my mom's formal gown! The only difference was that today the dress is longer. Today, she wears a golden robe with it. *Huh, I never knew that the dress and crown would change as you get older.*

I looked down at my mom's feet and saw her iconic green combat heels that had wrap-around vines and live blooming poppies. They let off her deadly poppy smell, even when she wasn't wearing her shoes. Her mask also had live poppies, which gave out an even stronger smell, so she didn't wear it all the time.

She wore a crown. It was one I'd seen with pure rubies and emeralds. The crown was made by the original owner of the prehistoric ANW, Haita Hope. It was set with diamonds in the twelfth century, which were then replaced as it got older. It was passed on to Giovanna in the eighteenth century. She set it with blood-red rubies and bright green emeralds that she had found in a mine.

So, no matter how much we changed ANW, it really wasn't ours until three centuries ago.

My grandmother called out from the back, "Rachel Lemondola, now known as Poppy, you are the next leader of ANW! Your

91

power is the deadly poppies you hold, which can knock out anyone coming your way. You now hold the sacred tiara that has been in our family for three hundred years. Protect our organization with care, and keep it going in your family proudly!"

Even though the past version of my aunt looked happy, I could sense something else: Jealousy. She twisted her hands and looked the other way.

Ariana's black hair magically shortened into a bob. Her mask had dead rose petals, and I could almost smell the roses from where I was, even though this was just a memory. Her dress was made of layers of fabric, like a pile of rose petals. She wore bracelets made of thorns and red flats. She had a necklace with a charm shaped like a rose.

"Ariana, your codename is Rose, and you have the power to heal with the touch of your necklace!" my grandmother called out. The past version of my aunt looked happy, but she kept looking at my mother's crown.

The last step for the girls was to level up and accept their weapons. They sat in a room with my grandma, an elderly man, and an elderly woman. My grandma had tears in her eyes.

"Today is the day I get to see my two daughters reach their final stage in ANW. ANW was created over five hundred years ago by the great Hatia Hope and passed down to Giovanna Lemondola, who founded this version of ANW.

"Today, my daughters level up to the prestigious level three and become full assassins: my oldest, Rachel, as well as my youngest, the most promising ANW of all time, Ariana. Ariana has proven at eleven that she is more than ready to become one of us." My aunt and mom went up and received the blessings of the woman, the man, and my grandma. Next, they earned their own cards.

"Wait, they're not being handed badges," I said aloud.

"Your mother made the badges when she was made leader. In the twenty-first century, assassins have to be more careful than ever. The badges identified an assassin if they were hurt. A...friend told me about them every time he was in ANW," Ariana said. She smiled sadly and stared at her younger self and my mom.

I decided to stop talking and watch the rest of the memory. My favorite part was when my aunt and mother swapped their weapons for something new. The bow and arrows were gone, and before you knew it, my aunt grabbed a laser gun, and my mom picked a dagger.

"Go, now," my grandmother told them. "Tomorrow, you will pick your life group and learn their true identities, which you will stick with as long as you are part of ANW."

"Unfortunately, for me, tomorrow never came," my aunt said.

Suddenly, the scene got blurry, like somebody was crying through it. The big TV paused and turned off.

My aunt had started crying. Suddenly, the void, the sofa, and the TV disappeared.

"I can't, Clara. I can't do this. I'll break down through the next half," she sobbed.

"You don't have to right now, but I need to know the truth someday," I said.

We were back in the little room and I wondered how much time had passed. I was shocked when I looked at the clock and saw it had only been two minutes.

"I will tell you the rest of the story when I get back, and maybe even say hello to your mother, if she will let me back in." My aunt stopped crying and straightened up. "I need to help your friends get ready and rest. I will show you something that will help you get your strength back in the morning. Then, you can tell me why you are going this way. First, take a shower, and when you get back, I will place some food and clothes on your bed. Eat and sleep. You will need your rest. Goodnight, my niece," my aunt said in her sweet and warm voice.

I started to look for the bathroom, when my aunt talked to me again.

"Oh, and please, call me Ari. Ariana seems a mouthful, dontcha think?" Aunt Ari smiled.

I headed to the bathroom. I felt overwhelmed. I forgot about R and A. I just hoped they ate and slept peacefully. I had so many questions in my head they felt like bombs waiting to go off any second.

This lady was my aunt? How did she end up here? Was she married?

I shook off the questions and headed into the shower. The hot water warmed me and the color came into my skin. I dried off, and went into the guest room. The room had a chalkboard with my name written on it. Inside, I found white sweatpants and a shirt waiting for me. It felt good to wear something that didn't have blood, soot, or dirt on it. I ate a dinner of rice pudding and pizza. The dinner had been placed on the nightstand.

I rested my head on the pillow and fell asleep at once.

CHAPTER 18
SPY MODE ACTIVATED

DAMIEN

"You're kidding, right?" I asked Arthur nervously. I prayed in my head that the guy was joking, but his face gave it away.

"I wish, Mr. Richards." Arthur shook his head and cracked his knuckles.

"Well, do you have any idea how to get out of here?" I asked.

"As a matter of fact, I do! I remember there's a back entrance, and we can just slip through it. The only problem is that to get to it, we need to sneak by two dozen execs and get through a spike-filled pit." He counted the dangers on his fingers.

"So, we're trapped."

He nodded.

I groaned and remembered that I had my bookmark and pulled it out. Arthur looked confused at the bookmark.

"What are we supposed to do with that?" he asked.

I explained that all I had to do was tug the ribbon and it would turn the bookmark into a dagger. He looked amazed.

"Better than when I was in ANW," he said aloud. "Then, we had swords that weighed more than you do."

I snickered.

I knew that Poppy got rid of the swords even before I joined. Although it would be cute to see five-year-olds holding them.

I grabbed my backpack and took a long look at it. I gulped. This was the last thing I should be thinking of, but my backpack had seen its last days. And as much as I wanted to ask my mom to buy a new one, I really didn't want to explain how I broke it in the first place.

Well, future me will have to deal with that. If future me lives through this.

"Stop worrying, boy!" Arthur barked. "You made it this far; you're going to get through this."

"Wait, is your ANW power mind-reading?"

"Nope. I never got my powers, but even a level one could figure out what you're thinking, Damien." He smiled weakly. "Chill, it's fine, but we should get going, since it could be dark outside."

I had to laugh at that. Skylock's—excuse me, *Shadow Man's*—palace was pitch black, with some torches here and there. I had no idea where my phone was. And I didn't even have my watch.

"Okay, yeah, we should really get going."

We went past the large metal door with spikes. We walked outside the tiger pit. Fluffy was sleeping. His paw was chained, and he looked very much in pain, even in his sleep.

Arthur shuddered. "I had really bad taste," he said.

"I gotta say, everything reeks in here except the tiger. I mean, I *hate* tigers, but I feel really bad for Fluffy." I put a hand on Arthur's shoulder. He smiled.

"You're correct. Maybe we should unlock his chains before we leave, so at least he won't have to suffer anymore. Besides, we're the good guys, right?"

"At this point, I honestly don't know anymore. I don't know *who* to trust," I sighed, yanking the cage open and unlocking Fluffy.

Arthur sighed and looked at me. "Kid, I know I haven't seen my niece in many years, but if she's like her mother and aunt, then she's amazing. Those women make mistakes like everybody else, and they're not very trusting, even with their loved ones. They come back stronger and more powerful every time, no matter the circumstances. Just take a look at Clara's mother. Her husband has no idea about this, and Rachel plans to make it stay that way. She does it because she loves him. The same thing goes for Clara. She *cares* for you." Arthur smiled.

I felt relieved. Sure, I'd only just met Arthur, not Skylock. I'd only known him for about an hour, but I had a feeling Clara and her family would like him, just like I do.

"Wait, when did you become Dr. Phil?" I laughed.

"I got tricks up my sleeves, kid," he said. "Now, let's get the heck out of here."

"I'm with you, Arthur." We walked for a bit, passing bodies, blood, and some rusted knives. Arthur geared up by picking up a couple knives. I felt weak, and I knew he did too.

I hadn't eaten for at least a day and a half. I wondered when Arthur had last had a decent meal. He snuck up behind the three execs who guarded a sacred room. He put his back against the wall, and signed for me to come with him.

When we peered out from behind the wall, we were face-to-face with an exec. We turned around, and two dozen execs stood right behind us.

We were trapped.

CHAPTER 19

STRANGERS ARE JUST FRIENDS YOU'VE MET, BUT DECIDED TO IGNORE

CLARA

I woke up to the sound of birds. The sun shone on my face. I sat up and listened, wondering if anybody was awake. I didn't hear anyone. I pulled on some leggings and a shirt my aunt had lent me. I crept out of the room and explored the house. It's not nosy if it's trying to help someone, as Nancy Drew would say. I totally respect that girl.

I pulled out my dagger. You never know how people are going to behave, especially when you work with the sweet-toothed and the backstabbers.

I put my mask on. I wasn't sure if R and A were going to walk into the room. I'm pretty sure my mom would get mad if we revealed our identities, even in the most dire of situations.

Most moms would get furious that their kid got in trouble at school. My mom would get furious if I let my true identity slip even to Damien. I don't blame her. I mean, that's the whole point of ANW.

Five rooms in the house are not normal. When I say normal, I'm talking about rooms like the bathroom, pool, living room... etc. The first of these was a greenhouse. I saw some radishes, carrots, and leeks. I walked up and down the rows of vegetables. I saw that one plant had not gotten water and that it was about to die. I grabbed the nearest watering can and watered it. I said a prayer for the little plant.

Next, the second strange room. To my surprise, it looked like a nursery. The walls were bright pink, and there were silver words painted on the wall: "I love you to the moon and back." There was an empty crib. Interesting. Although the room was pretty, it looked like it had been abandoned. The shelves were covered with dust, and the toys looked brand new. I could ask my aunt later, once we saved Damien.

I walked into the third strange room. This one had a desk and some other office supplies. I knew it was my aunt's office. The fourth room was a movie room, with cinema wallpaper and luxury seats. The movie *Five Feet Apart* was playing on the screen. I had just seen it. It was so sad.

I could tell my aunt must have felt sleepy during the movie and had gone to bed. There was a blanket and some popcorn on the floor.

The door of the fifth room didn't open. I saw a familiar sign on the door. It was the symbol of ANW—an arrow, a dagger, and a heart. The arrow represented war, the dagger stood for death, and the heart stood for compassion and loyalty. I knew this was one of the 10,000 doors around the world that assassins used. In my house, we have five of them. I wondered how to get in. Then I remembered. My mother had said that my key would open any special door. I took the key from my necklace and put it in the lock. The door slid open.

The room was a workout room! It was a heaven of punching bags, climbing rocks, and even a stepper with a built-in iPad! I raced around the whole room before I stopped at a nearby bench. I heard the door scrape open and threw my dagger toward the sound. A crash told me someone had caught it.

My aunt smiled and handed my knife back. "Your mother was always the curious one, the one who couldn't wait more than five seconds," she said. I was shocked.

"But you caught the dagger..." I stammered.

"Yes. Even though I left many years ago, I still have my muscle memory."

I heard the door open again and R and A burst in without their masks. They both blushed a fiery pink and stood speechless before they turned to my trying-not-to-laugh aunt. I couldn't figure them out.

After a couple seconds, I turned to A, the boy, who had cream-colored skin, brown eyes, and jet-black hair. He wore a black shirt with khaki pants. He had a pretty rainbow beaded bracelet on his wrist.

"Alvin? Is that you?" I said. I almost laughed. Of course A would be Alvin. Their personalities match, and I had always kept an eye on Alvin. He had perfect hand-eye coordination, and now I know why. It was because of his training with the bow and arrow.

"Yep, that's me. But who are you?" he asked. He was so calm, I swear he thought I was asking him where the nearest bathroom was.

Before I answered, I turned to the girl. She had tussock-colored skin, with brown hair and purple highlights. I only knew the exact color of the girl's skin because I saw the same mixture at Home Depot last week on a paint jar.

My face burned. I felt like I was going to faint. Did it have to be *her*? The girl wore a white layered top with black pants, and she held a knife. Her hands shook.

"Raina Waterhouse. I heard you snitched on one of my friends today, Clara Lemondola," I said, crossing my arms.

"What's it to you? That brat deserved it," Raina replied. She blew her purple hair out of her face. She picked her nails and didn't look at me.

Alvin gulped and inched closer to my aunt.

"I'm Clara," I said. I tore off my mask and watched the shock on Alvin and Raina's faces.

"Clarissa? *You're* C?" Alvin asked. His jaw dropped.

"Yes, please, for the love of ANW, just call me Clara."

Even Raina looked taken aback. "I thought girls like you couldn't handle grime and blood," she said.

"Right, and I thought snitches weren't tolerated at ANW." This time, Raina and Aunt Ari looked taken aback.

"Listen, Clara," said Aunt Ari. "What I did was wrong and stupid. I was jealous and young. My mother, your grandmother, thought I was capable of leveling up. She wasn't right. Now, I have to make up for my mistakes, if you will let me. Like your mother always said, Second chances are rare."

Raina interjected. "Clara, you hate me, I get it. I don't exactly.... admire you either, but your aunt here's got a point. Honestly, I never wanted to hurt you. You just remind me of someone who ruined my life forever."

"I don't understand that feeling, Raina, but maybe I understand where your anger's coming from. My supposed best friend has got a lot of explaining to do," I softened. "Aunt Ari, you...you are right.

Mom always says that second chances should be given out when deserved. It's one of her favorite sayings. Thank you. Now I know I can trust you, at least enough to help us."

"I will cherish that trust," Aunt Ari smiled. Raina smiled too. Someone sniffled. Alvin rubbed his eyes.

"Are you *crying?*" Raina laughed.

"Noooo." Alvin wiped his eyes.

Aunt Ari muttered, "I need coffee after all this drama." She left the training room.

Alvin opened his mouth to say something, but Raina put a hand over it. "Before you say something stupid," she said, "I need more information. What do we do now that you're fine, Clarissa? Not that I care anyway. Alvin's not going to want to leave yet and look like a selfish coward."

Well, Raina had gone back to her usual self, but now I knew that there was a kind person underneath her hard cover. I just had to dig in to open her up.

Alvin looked like he was about to say something snarky, but he stopped at Raina's glare.

"I guess ask Aunt Ari. Maybe she'll have more ideas of how to approach Skylock after she has her coffee. After all, she *is* the only person who's ever pulled the wool over ANW's eyes and betrayed them," I sighed.

We walked over to the front room where my aunt was sitting, drinking coffee. Don't ask me how a person could make coffee that fast, because I honestly don't know.

"So, what are you doing here anyway, Clara?" Aunt Ari asked. "Your mom didn't send you to visit me."

I told her my story, and when I got to the part where the executioners got me, her eyes grew wide. She spluttered her coffee all over me. "Are you serious? You nearly got killed?"

"What did you expect? That we were playing with puppies and kittens? We're *assassins*, not animal shelter workers!" Raina said.

Ari glared at Raina.

"What do we do next, Ms. Velez?" Alvin asked.

"What do you mean? I thought you got an address for Skylock's palace," Ari replied.

"Here's the thing: My mom was pretty vague with the address, and she just gave me some coordinates. She said that Skylock's palace was around this area, but it kept changing locations. One year, it was inside a restaurant, the next, inside an abandoned hotel. Surprisingly, I checked the coordinates. It's about ten miles from here, except when I checked Google Maps, there's nothing there, just flat land," I said.

Ariana thought for a minute. Then, she brightened. She seemed to have an idea. "There *is* an old fort about ten miles from here. I pass it every day when I go to work," she said. "I'm guessing we check there first for Skylock. That sounds like an ideal spot where he would hide out, considering what you've told me."

She told us to pack what we needed.

I went back into the guest room and took off my coffee-stained shirt. I grabbed my messenger bag. I filled it with some clothes I borrowed from my aunt, my knife, a hairbrush, and some stink bombs. You never know when they will come in handy.

I scanned my card and changed into a fresh ANW uniform. Smiling into the mirror, I walked to the front door, where Aunt Ari, Alvin, and Raina stood.

Raina had on her tattered uniform, while Alvin wore a fresh suit. He just nodded at me. Both had their masks on. Aunt Ari wore a biker's jacket, a white shirt, and jeans. I grinned. She was the total opposite of my mom.

"This is more like it," my aunt said. "I couldn't wear it because I wanted to hide myself from the world so I wouldn't be spotted by an enemy.

"Are you ready?" I asked Raina and Alvin. They shared a look and nodded. "There's no going back."

CHAPTER 20
THE FASTEST REUNION
I HAVE SEEN IN MY LIFE

CLARA

Even though the execs couldn't reach us in the car, everyone was on alert. Alvin checked his watch, Raina kept adjusting her bag, and my aunt looked around each time we hit a red light. We were the first underage assassins on a mission, the first to mess with Skylock and his gang.

Alvin turned pale. Raina started shivering and pointing. I looked at where she was pointing. On top of a small hill, there was a mansion. Inside, there were a lot of execs circling two people. It was Damien and a man I didn't recognize. My aunt saw them, and she drove right up the hill at about 100 miles per hour.

We held on and got ready to jump out of the car. At the very top, she stopped the car and got out. We followed right behind her. Each of us had only one weapon. Damien saw me, and his face lit up. I put a finger to my lips and told him to be quiet. He nodded.

Alvin hid in a spot north of the execs, Raina was to the south, Aunt Ari to the west, and I was to the east. I signaled for Aunt Ari to jump out and start fighting. She knew what to do and gave a piercing whistle. We all jumped out and joined her.

Alvin held out his hand, and I jumped on it. The wind blew in my hair. I face-kicked some execs and somersaulted backwards. I swung Raina by the hand and let go. She dodged execs that were in her way, and knocked out all the execs in her path.

Aunt Ari and Alvin did the signature ANW tango move. It was basically just tango. They twirled each other so much that if I was doing that move I would have already barfed. This tango dance is special, though. Whenever the partner dips the dancer, the dancer has a blow dart ready to shoot at the nearest exec. The dart makes a person fall unconscious for two hours—but it doesn't kill them. Remember, only in the most dire situations are we allowed to kill.

Don't kill? So why are we called assassins? Like I said from the very start, assassins are not what my grandma intended us to be called as, but it's a better name than superheroes. Superheroes don't usually kill people, and they end up in the spotlight the whole time. I don't think I could handle that type of pressure as an assassin. In the end, I think people who saw us in action and barely escaped creatively gave us the name "assassins." At least the press doesn't follow us around like they would if we were superheroes. I get enough news coverage as Clara Lemondola. I don't need the same attention as C.

Aunt Ari and Alvin finished off all the execs in each of their zones. We fought our way to the edge of the ring of execs, when I heard the man next to Damien cry out. He had been shot. We ran to him. Damien held him in an awkward way. When I took a closer look, I recognized Skylock. Something was off about him. His eyes looked familiar. I'd never seen his eyes since he usually wore sunglasses.

"Damien, that's Skylock! Why are you saving him? He's our enemy!" I yelled.

"Clara, meet Arthur Wells, your uncle. He was brainwashed into becoming Skylock," Damien said.

I was shocked. His face was bruised so badly that I could only see his eyes. The sunglasses had hidden his face as Skylock. I saw that my aunt was horrified. Arthur is her husband. He had just been shot.

"Arthur, is that you?" she cried.

My uncle nodded. This man could die if we didn't get him treatment. My aunt took out a bottle that looked like it had a tiny bit of some fluid inside. "This is a healing potion. It can cure him!" She put the drops into his mouth. My uncle got up. We all sighed with relief.

"You have got to give me that healing potion, along with the mask remover," I said.

"When you're more responsible, Clarissa," my aunt playfully bonked my nose.

Arthur hugged my aunt for about ten minutes. They talked quietly. Damien came up to me. I pretended to look mad. I crossed my arms. He smiled.

"Same old Clara," he said. I couldn't help from smiling.

My uncle looked up. It was sundown. The man who brainwashed my uncle could strike ANW anytime now that we were out of the way.

"I suggest we go now," my uncle said.

"If I know your mom, she will be worried sick," my aunt said.

Since we had walked all the way, it was a five-hour journey driving home from Skylock's palace.

"Why did you walk all this way?" Damien teased me. He knew the answer perfectly well, as did every assassin. Car rides are lethal.

"Really?" I put my hands on my hips, and then kicked Damien's shin. He hobbled in pain and groaned.

"*That* was for not telling me you're an assassin," I said. Then I gave him a hug. He electrocuted for a second and hugged me right back. "This is for scaring me half to death and making me have to come save you with two not-so-random strangers."

112

"Wait, two not-so-random strangers? Who are they?" he asked.

I called Raina and Alvin over. They looked super uncomfortable, but I really wanted to thank them for helping me.

"Raina! Alvin! How are you guys doing? How's ANW treating you?" Damien said.

"Actually, we're enjoying it. Thanks for asking, Richards," Raina said, before Alvin could get a word in. She gave Damien a small grin, and turned to talk to Aunt Ari.

I started to run behind Raina to punch her, when Alvin and Damien held me by both arms.

"I can't believe she didn't even look at me when I said hi to her. She talks to Damien like he knew her all his life," I fumed.

Alvin let go of my hand and followed Raina. Damien hugged me.

"I can't let you go until I punish you for not telling me that *you're* an assassin, Clara," Damien said. "What do you choose? Hugs or shin kicks?"

I backed away. Damien was really strong with his shin kicks, whether he was mad at somebody or not.

"Fine, deadly hugs it is," I said. Damien hugged me really hard.

He whispered in my ear. "Anyway, I'm glad you're back."

So am I.

CHAPTER 21
CHAOS IN SLOW MOTION

DAMIEN

"What if we all teleported?" I asked Clara. "One of us could hold Arthur, and the other could hold your aunt."

Clara's eyes lit up. She shared the idea with Arthur and Mrs. Velez. They nodded in agreement.

"That would save us the five-hour drive," Arthur said.

I held Arthur while Clara took her aunt. Raina and Alvin held each other and then held Clara's aunt. Clara pulled out her card, as I did mine, and Raina and Alvin drew theirs. We all had to channel the magic in our cards, since they connected with us. ANW rarely uses tech. Besides, that only came in the last few centuries. Imagine how Giovanna teleported. That's exactly how we are going to do it. Before I go ahead, you must be wondering: Why didn't Clara just teleport?

Now, the only reason Clara walked to Skylock's palace was because teleportation should never be done unaccompanied unless you're with a level three for the whole ride. I guess two older ANW assassins made us eligible to travel.

The magic in our cards opened a hole. It swirled with holographic colors. We jumped into the hole holding hands.

I landed on the ground. We were just outside Clara's house. It was dark, but an eerie glow came from the forest behind the house. I turned to Clara. "What is going on?" She must have been wondering the same thing.

Arthur and Clara's aunt saw it too. We all ran. I scanned on my mask and went in.

I let Arthur and Ariana in. All of us just stared. The ANW grounds were on fire. I could see ANW assassins fighting men and women dressed in black wearing the familiar brown eagle badge.

Rain, a senior ANW, ran up to us. She showered water at dozens of execs while she ran. "C, your mother is fighting, you should go help her," she said, out of breath.

"Fighting what?" Clara asked. I looked at her carefully. Clara's hands were shaking more than an avalanche, and her face had turned ghost white.

116

"Fighting 10,000 execs. The Shadow Man released all his troops on us. We're all dead."

TO BE CONTINUED...

ABOUT THE AUTHOR

Nirmani Walpola is a part-time author, part-time reader, and a full-time Sri Lankan teenager. This is her very first book, and she encourages all young people to write their hearts out, just like she did. She lives in Texas with her two amazing sisters and her one-of-a-kind parents. Follow Nirmani on Instagram

@THEMIDNIGHTWARRIORS

ACKNOWLEDGMENTS

Wow. It's been a long journey, and hopefully, it's just the beginning.

It's time to say thank you to the people who matter most, my favorite part in a book.

To Mr. Isaac Peterson, Dr. Linda Tucker, and Dr. Jessica Hammerman, thank you for taking my book and working with it. I am so grateful and honored that I am working with Emerald Books and can't wait to see what's in the future with you guys!

To everybody who supported my book at Inkshares, thank you. Give yourselves a pat on the back. You deserve it.

To all my family friends, my mom's friends, and my dad's friends, thank you for all the books you bought and advice you gave.

To all 185 agencies that I reached to out last year to represent my book: Thank you for passing it on because each denied query made me stronger. Thanks for being part of The Midnight Warriors' journey.

To Rachel Renee Russell, Soman Chainani, Wendelin Van Draanen, Rick Riordan, and Victoria Aveyard: I don't know if you will ever see this, but thank you for inspiring me to write this book. Keep inspiring kids like me around the world.

To my 11½-year-old self, you had no idea that what began as a dare after falling asleep in second period yoga would turn into this book. Thank you for being the persistent girl you are and finishing!

To the library, Disney Plus, Netflix, and all the movies/series that inspire me, the world of TMW wouldn't have existed without you.

To the Sri Lankan kids, Rayani, Nethumi, Ayami, Senuth, and Mihiri, you guys are the first I would venture into ANW with. Thanks for reading and supporting me.

To Ms. Fay and Mrs. Fuhrman, thanks for making writing so much fun in fourth grade. I would have never made it without you.

To Mrs. York, what can I say? Thanks for inspiring five-year-old me to read by reading a chapter of Junie B. Jones every day. Thanks for leading me to one of life's greatest wonders: reading.

To Isa, Livia, Siena, Marlene, Angela, Purvi, and Sanaya, thanks for being my beta readers and supporters from Day 1.

To dear Chunni, Mayee, and Chuti Mayee, hope you're proud of your Loku Akka. I can't wait until all of you are old enough to read my book. Thanks for being the most amazing cousins ever.

To mami and nandi, you are the best aunt and uncle a niece can have. Thank you for always having my back.

To my grandparents, Acha, Seeya, Achiammi, and Seeya, thank you for calling up everybody and telling them about my book. Thanks for always picking up my FaceTime calls and watching me drone on and on about my book. You're the grandparents a granddaughter can only wish for.

To Nuwani, my little sis by only 18 months: Nangi, thanks for being that one person who will torture me and love me at the same time. You were my first TMW lover and critic. Thanks for being my series watching partner, wonderful artist, and Webtoon reading comrade.

To Punchi, my little sister. It's amazing how many questions you ask every day, and how I get to see the world from your 8-year-old eyes. Thanks for being my sister. You deserve the world.

To my dad, Thathi, I can't even say how lucky I am to get to be your daughter. Thank you for teaching me to live in this world. Thank you for all those songs you taught me. Thanks for all the times you patiently heard me complain about everything in life. Thanks for being my #1 cheerleader. I'll always be your chuti duwa.

To my mom, Ammi, thank you. Thank you for answering my questions about growing up, and taking everything I said seriously. Thank you for teaching me to properly behave, and making the best food ever. Thank you for being there as my emotional support. I don't know what I'd ever do without you. Love you Ammi, your Kuku Ba.

Made in the USA
Coppell, TX
26 July 2021